What am I getting into here? Cat wondered incredulously.

Some kind of business arrangement controlled by dates and logistics—efficient, but passionless?

No, she thought, remembering Liam's smile and the sudden, sensuous glint in his eyes that had so rocked her. Certainly not passionless, but maybe not very romantic, either.

If she was honest, she realized, she'd never considered the practical details of her idea until this very moment. But Liam had brought them home to her, loud and clear. She fell suddenly cold, and pulled the folds of the robe around her.

I should have tempted him to stay— used my own powers of persuasion, she thought.

And she would, next time…

MISTRESS
TO A
MILLIONAIRE

*She's his in the bedroom,
but he can't buy her love.*

The ultimate fantasy becomes a reality.

Live the dream with more
MISTRESS TO A MILLIONAIRE titles
by some of your much-loved
Harlequin Presents® authors.

Watch for more titles throughout 2005!

Sara Craven

MISTRESS AT A PRICE

MISTRESS
TO A
MILLIONAIRE

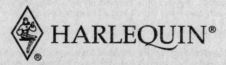

HARLEQUIN®

TORONTO • NEW YORK • LONDON
AMSTERDAM • PARIS • SYDNEY • HAMBURG
STOCKHOLM • ATHENS • TOKYO • MILAN • MADRID
PRAGUE • WARSAW • BUDAPEST • AUCKLAND

ISBN 0-373-12471-6

MISTRESS AT A PRICE

First North American Publication 2005.

This edition published by arrangement with Harlequin Books S.A.

www.eHarlequin.com

Printed in U.S.A.

PROLOGUE

September

THE bathroom was lit by candles, their flames burning steadily in the warm still air.

She tilted the flask of fragrant oil and added a few drops to the steaming water in the deep tub, drawing a deep, appreciative breath as the smoky scent of lilies reached her.

A glass of chilled white wine was waiting on the small table beside the bath, with a tall, slender vase of freesias. Music was drifting in from the bedroom next door—a sultry Latin beat, quietly and insistently sexy.

Perfect, she thought, pinning her hair into a loose coil on top of her head, then untying the sash of her silk robe and letting it fall to the ground. She stepped into the water, leaning back against the little neck pillow with a brief sigh of satisfaction, letting her whole body relax by inches. Feeling the tensions of the day slowly disappear. To be replaced by a different sort of excitement.

She picked up her wine glass and sipped. Not long to wait now. Only half an hour—forty minutes at the most—to complete this precious ritual, and be waiting—and oh, so ready. She laughed softly in anticipation.

The soap was scented with lilies too. She worked it into a gentle lather and began to apply it to her skin, taking her time, her senses tingling in anticipation of the moment when other hands would touch her body—other fingers caress her sensitised flesh.

She soaped one smooth, slender leg and then the other, lifting each of them clear out of the water and surveying them critically, admiring the pearly sheen of the polish on her toe-nails.

Her belly was as flat as she could wish, and her hips were slim but gently rounded. All in all, she was in good shape.

She was taking better care of her body these days, she reminded herself. She ate sensibly and went regularly to the gym.

All I ever needed, she thought, slanting a secret smile, was the right motivation.

'You look terrific,' a male colleague had remarked over lunch, his eyes appraising. 'Don't tell me you're in love.'

'I won't,' she'd retorted crisply. 'Because I'm not.'

She wondered now what he'd have said if she'd told him the truth. Let him in on her secret night-times—this hedonistic, sensual bargain that gave her all the pleasure of love but none of the pain.

Yet there might eventually be pain, she supposed. If one of them decided it was time to part before the other was ready.

But that wasn't a thought that need trouble her tonight. Not on the very brink of his arrival.

She cupped water in her hands and poured it over her shoulders, letting it cascade down her taut breasts. Watching the droplets clustering on her rosy nipples. Feeling the breath catch in her throat as she imagined his mouth capturing them.

Not long now, she told herself, and, as if on cue, her mobile phone rang.

Her mouth curved in delight as she checked the caller.

'Welcome back,' she said softly, her tone faintly teasing. 'You seem to have been away for ever.'

She leaned back, her smile widening as she listened. 'You'll be here in twenty minutes? That's terrific.'

She paused, then added huskily, 'But hurry—please. Because I'm waiting for you…'

CHAPTER ONE

IT WAS a beautiful day for a wedding, Cat Adamson thought as she descended the steps of the hotel terrace and began to walk slowly across the lawns towards the lake.

That was, of course, if you liked weddings, which Cat most assuredly did not. And her cousin Belinda's nuptials were priming themselves to head the list as the worst ever.

What a relief, she told herself wryly, to breathe fresh air for a while instead of the violent clash of expensive designer scents. And how wonderful to hear actual birdsong instead of the magpie clamour of high-pitched voices, interspersed with the boom of male conversation and the intrusion of over-loud laughter.

No one, she thought, had noticed her leave the reception.

Not the bride, her eyes narrowing to suspicious slits as she watched Freddie, her new husband, chat up the chief bridesmaid with far too much enjoyment.

Not the bride's father, Cat's Uncle Robert, who had earlier made an emotional speech on the sanctity of marriage, regardless of the fact that he'd been having an affair with his secretary for the past year. Nor her much loved Aunt Susan, who'd stood beside him like a statue throughout his remarks, staring down at the floor, her expression unreadable.

And certainly not Cat's own parents, who had both arrived, to the excitement of the other guests, with their latest in a long line of alternative partners, and who were stonily pretending to ignore each other from opposite ends of the room.

A happy state of affairs which could, however, change at any moment.

When last seen, her father had been tight-lipped and her

mother had had bright spots of colour in her face and been tapping her foot. Not good signs.

But then, as Cat knew to her cost, they were both professional actors with volatile personalities, and there were times when any stage would do. And any audience.

She could remember school prize-givings and sports days which had left her shaking with tension, as well as a really hideous scene at her eighteenth birthday party.

So why should their only niece's wedding be spared?

Since their split-up ten years ago, when Cat was still in her early teens, her father and mother had both remarried and divorced twice. And it looked as if they were each planning another danger trip into the rocky shoals of matrimony, although it was anyone's guess how long this latest foray would last, she thought, grimacing.

As David Adamson had sauntered in, his trophy blonde on his arm, Cat had found herself detained by her mother, her manicured and polished nails digging painfully into her arm.

'What the hell is your father doing here?' she demanded. 'I accepted this invitation on the sole understanding that he would be in California.'

Cat shrugged, detaching the sleeve of her crêpe de chine jacket from her mother's grasp. 'Filming ended early,' she returned. 'And he is Uncle Robert's only brother. Naturally he was going to be here if he could.'

'And with his latest tart, I see.' Vanessa Carlton gave a small brittle laugh. 'My God, she's about your age.'

'I suppose he could say the same of your choice of escort,' Cat said evenly, trying to ignore the fact that the gentleman in question—tall, bronzed, with perfect teeth that he liked people to know about—was blowing an extravagant kiss at her mother.

'There's no comparison,' Vanessa denied indignantly. 'Gil and I are in love—deeply and sincerely. He says he has always been drawn to older, more sophisticated women. He likes—maturity.'

Cat's lips tightened. 'Really? Then I hope he's not around when you start throwing things.'

Vanessa gave her a fulminating look. 'I admit I've made my mistakes,' she said. 'But I see now that any other relationships in the past were simply—tragic mistakes. But then,' she added angrily, 'you've always taken your father's side.'

Before Cat could reply her mother had beckoned to Gil and set off determinedly round the room, towing him in her wake.

Leaving Cat to make her escape through the open French windows. Once outside, she drew a deep, shaking breath. That was one of the hardest things to bear—the constant accusations that she supported one parent more than the other.

Because it was simply not true. She'd done her best always—*always* to be even-handed. Often under very difficult circumstances.

She wished now that she'd turned down the entire invitation to the wedding, and not just Belinda's reluctant invitation for her to be one of the bridesmaids. At least she'd had the sense to avoid that.

She couldn't altogether blame her cousin for the undercurrent of hostility which had always soured their relationship. Belinda, too, was an only child, and had clearly resented Cat's regular invasion of her family circle, even though she must have been aware there was nowhere else for her to go.

Even before the divorce David and Vanessa had been missing a lot of the time, either on location or touring in various plays. Although Cat could remember an idyllic year at Stratford, where she'd joined them during her holidays from boarding school. And she had been with them during long runs in West End plays too.

Their separation and divorce had sent a seismic shock through the acting world, quite apart from the devastating effect on Cat herself.

There'd always been rows—tantrums, shouting and slammed doors—but followed by equally full-blooded reconciliations.

That last time, however, there had been no displays of histrionics, just a terrible quietness. And then, as if a switch had been thrown, they'd both plunged feverishly back into their separate careers and new much-vaunted relationships.

From then on Cat had owed what remained of her childhood stability to Uncle Robert and Aunt Susan. In spite of her problems with Belinda, their big, rambling house had seemed an oasis of security in her shaken world.

Which had made it even harder to bear, she thought sadly, when she'd spotted her uncle a few months ago at a corner table in a smart London restaurant, exchanging playful forkfuls of food and lingering glances with a much younger woman.

Perhaps he'd always been more like her father than she'd realised, she told herself with real regret, and this affair with his secretary was not the first time he'd strayed.

Looking back, she could pinpoint other strains and tensions in the household which she'd been too young to understand. Or maybe she'd simply been too immersed in her own shock and bewilderment at her parents' parting to care.

After all, that had been the time when she'd learned about being alone, and the dangers of relying on other people for happiness.

On today's performances, she thought, wincing, why would anyone wish to be married—ever? When betrayal and heartbreak seemed to be forever waiting in ambush.

It's togetherness that seems to kill the thing off, she told herself broodingly. Maybe familiarity does breed contempt, after all.

Which was why she'd always retreated from any serious commitment, especially when moving in together had been suggested.

First you find somewhere to rent together, she thought, and then you get a joint mortgage, to be closely followed by an engagement party, and a trip down the aisle in a meringue like Belinda's.

But I can't do that. I am never, ever going to be caught in that trap. To hitch my wagon to one particular star when all the evidence suggests it doesn't work.

Yet, if she was honest, celibacy had no great appeal either.

I don't believe in 'happy ever after', she thought. But what's wrong with 'happy for now'?

The rest of her life was in order. She had an absorbing career, a terrific flat, and a pleasant social life.

So surely it should be possible to compromise somehow over the love thing? Find a relationship where she could still maintain a distance—enjoy her own space. And make it clear that it was the here and now that interested her, and not the future.

There was a faint breeze coming from the water as she reached the lake's edge. It tousled her pale blonde hair, blowing the silky strands across her face. Impatiently Cat tried to rake them back into their usual layered bob, her attention caught by a moorhen proceeding with her chicks in a sedate convoy towards the reeds.

Life, she thought, must be so simple for moorhens. She was about to step forward for a better look when somewhere near at hand a man suddenly spoke, breaking into her consciousness.

'I really don't advise that.' His voice was low pitched and cool, with a note of amusement in its depths.

Cat turned sharply, shaken by the realisation that she had unsuspected company, her brows snapping into a frown at having her peace suddenly disturbed.

No wonder she hadn't noticed him. Although he was only a few yards away, he was standing half hidden in the shade of a weeping willow, one shoulder propped negligently against its slender trunk.

As he moved forward, pushing aside the trailing branches, Cat saw that he was tall and lean-hipped. A faded red polo shirt set off powerful shoulders, and his long legs were encased in shabby cream denims.

His face and forearms were tanned, and his thick dark hair curled slightly, yet he wasn't handsome in any conventional sense. His high-bridged nose was too thin, and the lids that shaded his grey-green eyes were too heavy for that. But his mouth was well defined and humorous, with a faintly sensual curve to its lower lip.

Absorbing this, Cat felt jolted by a sudden stab of recognition. Which was ludicrous, she thought, dry-mouthed. Because she'd never seen this man before in her life.

If I had, she told herself, drawing a deep, unsteady breath, I'd remember it. My God, but I would.

She realised that he was studying her in turn, his own brows drawn together in faint bewilderment, as if he too was trying to place her in some context.

She was aware of the slow, strained thud of her own heartbeat. The sunlit silence seemed to enclose them, locking them together into a golden web. The deep breath she drew sounded like a sigh.

Then, somewhere close at hand, a bird sounded a note, long and piercingly sweet.

Breaking the strange spell that had trapped her and bringing her sharply back to reality. She stiffened—instantly and defensively.

'Do you usually hand out unwanted advice to complete strangers?' She kept her tone curt.

'You're pretty near the edge, and the mud is treacherous where you're standing.' He shrugged, apparently unfazed by her abruptness. 'I wouldn't like you to slip and fall on your back—or worse.'

'Thank you,' she said. 'But I'm quite capable of looking after myself. You really don't need to be concerned.'

He'd halted a few feet away, hands on hips. 'It's pure self-interest, I promise you.' His expression was deadpan. 'If you fell in, I'd feel obliged to rescue you, and that water is freezing and full of weeds. Besides,' he added, subjecting her ivory slip dress and the filmy turquoise and ivory jacket she wore over it to another lingering appraisal, 'this wedding gear of yours clearly cost someone an arm and a leg. It would be a pity to spoil it.'

Cat's mouth tightened. 'Actually, I pay for my own clothes.' She frowned. 'And how do you know I'm at a wedding, anyway?'

He said drily, 'Well, you're clearly not dressed for a stroll in the countryside. Besides, I saw cars arriving earlier, done up with flowers and ribbons, plus girl in crinoline with veil looking furious. The usual stuff.'

He paused. 'So what role are you playing in all this? Matron of honour?'

'You're not as observant as you think.' She held up bare hands in a challenge she immediately regretted. 'I'm not married.'

'That doesn't necessarily follow,' he returned. 'Wedding rings might not be politically correct this month.'

She hesitated. 'I'm simply the bride's cousin. Just another guest.' She made a business of looking at her watch. 'And I really should be getting back now.'

'Why the sudden haste to go?' His tone was lazy but his eyes were intent. She could feel them examining her, with all the intimacy of a touch, and felt her throat tighten in mingled alarm and excitement.

'You wandered down here as if you had all the time in the world,' he went on.

'Because,' Cat said tautly. 'Things are quite tricky enough back there without me causing offence by staging a disappearing act.'

'Although you'd like to.' It was a statement, not a question. 'So, what's the problem? Got a secret yen for the groom?'

'God—no!' The denial was startled out of her.

'Well, that came from the heart.' His mouth slanted into a wry grin. 'What's wrong with him?'

Now was the moment to tell him politely it was none of

his business and go, thought Cat. Leave immediately, with no looking back.

So how was it she heard herself answering? 'He plays rugby all winter, cricket all summer, has too much money and a roving eye. Plus he drinks far more than he should, and is already overweight.'

He whistled appreciatively. 'You paint with words. No wonder the bride was looking so cross. Couldn't you have done her a favour and produced a just impediment?'

'I don't think she'd have thanked me,' Cat said drily. 'Even if he has been leering down her best friend's cleavage all through the reception.'

His brows rose. 'Have they cut the cake yet? If not, I'd watch what she does with the knife.'

Cat realised her mouth was twitching, and tried to control it. 'It's not funny. And I really don't know why I've told you all this, anyway,' she added frankly.

'Because you needed someone to talk to,' he said. 'And I happened to be here.'

'Well, it's very disloyal of me,' she said. 'And indiscreet. So, it would be kind of you to—put the whole thing out of your mind.'

'All duly forgotten,' he said. 'Except, of course, for meeting you,' he added thoughtfully. 'You can't really expect me to relegate that to some mental dustbin. That's too much to ask.'

'But we haven't met,' she said. 'Not really.' Oh, God, if he'd only stop looking at her like that. She could feel a languid warmth invading her that had nothing to do with the heat of the day. And instinct told her that it spelled danger—a complication that she didn't need.

'It's just been a chance encounter,' she continued hastily. 'And it's over now, anyway. I—I'm sure you have things to do.'

'Such as?'

'Well…' Cat gave his shirt and jeans a dubious look. 'You do work here, don't you?'

'Among other places,' he nodded.

'Then someone's paying for your time,' she said. 'And they might not be too pleased to find you…' She hesitated, searching for the right word.

'Loitering?' he supplied, his eyes glinting mockingly. 'With intent?'

She bit her lip. 'Something like that. I—I didn't think jobs were that easy to come by these days.'

'That rather depends on the job,' he told her softly. 'And whether or not you're an expert at what you do.'

'Which, naturally, you are,' Cat flashed back at him, with more haste than wisdom.

'I don't have many complaints.' He smiled at her slowly, letting her know without equivocation that this conversation had nothing to do with gainful employment.

Cat found herself stifling a gasp as her inner heat went suddenly soaring and her imagination ran momentarily wild. And he, she thought with shock, was as aware of that as she was herself.

'But it's good of you to care,' he added negligently.

She said carefully, as she got her breathing back under control, 'Actually, I don't give a damn what you do in your working hours or out of them. But I do wonder what the Durant hotel chain would say if they knew that one of their employees spent part of his working hours—harassing guests?'

His brows lifted. 'Is that what I'm doing?' he enquired sardonically. 'I hadn't realised. In that case, I'd better leave you in peace and return to my—er—duties, so that you can get back to the party of the century.' He turned, lifting a casual hand. 'Have a nice day.'

She was aware of ludicrously mixed feelings as he walked away. Yes, she'd found him both attractive and quite unbelievably unsettling, making it essential for the encounter to be brought to a brisk end before she said or did something genuinely stupid, but had it really been necessary to go into up-tight bitch mode instead?

Maybe, she thought wryly, because I know that at any other time or place I could have been very seriously tempted.

But now I have to get back to the reception and check that it hasn't descended into open warfare.

She made to turn and nearly overbalanced, arms flailing, as she realised, too late, that the slender high heel of one strappy turquoise sandal was stuck firmly in the mud.

Oh, God, she groaned inwardly, this is all I need.

She tried desperately to wriggle it free, but it wouldn't budge, and now her other heel appeared to be sinking too.

Of course she could always slip her feet out of her shoes and tiptoe to firmer ground, but it would be only too easy to slip.

And with her luck...

What she actually needed, she realised reluctantly, was assistance.

There was only one person in earshot who could provide that, and he was now some fifty yards away, and moving fast.

She put her hands to her mouth. 'Hey,' she called. 'Could you come back, please? I—I need help.'

He swung round and looked at her, and for one awful moment she was convinced he was simply going to shrug and walk on, leaving her there, stranded. Which, of course, would be the perfect revenge, she thought, simmering.

But then he began to make his way back, without particular hurry. He paused a few feet away, watching her, poker-faced. 'Having trouble?'

'As you see.' Cat bit her lip. 'And, yes, you warned me, so I only have myself to blame. But could you get me out of here, just the same?' She paused, waiting in vain for some move on his part—even some softening of his expression. Then added with some difficulty, 'Please?'

'I'd be delighted.' He walked over to her. 'Are you prepared to put your arm round my neck? Or will you have me arrested as well as fired?'

She flushed. 'I'm sorry about all that.' She tried a laugh. 'I'm—a little tense, that's all.'

She felt awkward and absurdly self-conscious as she did as she was bidden. Inadvertently her hand brushed his hair, and its crisp texture sent a shiver through her body.

He put his arm round her waist, and she felt his muscles bunch as he lifted her clear of her shoes, balancing her on his hip. She could feel the warmth of his body burning through her thin dress—and—even more troubling—the immediacy of her own response.

He smiled into her eyes. 'I'll do a trade with you,' he said softly. 'Have dinner with me tonight, and I'll not only rescue your footwear, Cinderella, but I'll also resist the temptation to dump you on your charming backside in the mud.'

Her arm tightened round his neck in pure alarm. 'You wouldn't dare.'

He allowed her to slip—just a fraction—and she gasped, half in panic and half at the increased intimacy of the contact, aware that her dress had ridden up round her thighs and that he knew it too.

'Well?' he said. 'Is it a deal?'

She was silent for a moment, her mind churning. Then, 'I suppose so,' she muttered.

'I've had more gracious acceptances.' There was a touch of wryness in his tone. 'But I guess I'll have to settle for what I can get—for now, at least.' He paused. 'Shall we say eight o'clock? They should have finished removing the bodies from the Banqueting Suite by then.'

Cat flushed, setting her mouth. 'I did ask you to forget what I said.'

'Impossible,' he said. 'But I will try not to refer to it again.'

'Thank you.' She hesitated. 'You're quite sure that you want to eat here?' She was genuinely surprised at the suggestion. The Anscote Manor Hotel was quietly luxurious, and it had a fine reputation for its food—with prices to match.

'You think they'll refuse to serve me?' He shook his head. 'They're quite democratic. There won't be a problem.'

Perhaps they even offered discount to staff, Cat thought, although it seemed unlikely on a busy summer evening. But if they were refused entry it would let her off the hook.

'Very well,' she acknowledged tonelessly. 'Eight it is, then.'

He carried her to a patch of dry grass and set her down, then went back for her shoes. He knelt, freeing each heel with great gentleness, then produced a handkerchief from his hip pocket and wiped them both carefully.

He brought them to her. 'Give me your foot,' he directed, sinking down on to one knee, and mutely she obeyed, resting a hand momentarily on his shoulder as he fitted the sandals back on for her. Finding, as she did so, that she was fighting an impulse to let her fingers stray over the crispness of his dark hair, or inside the collar of his shirt, and explore the taut muscularity of his shoulders. Feeling a strange trembling weakness stir deep inside her.

Oh, God, she told herself in a silent whisper. *I cannot—cannot allow this to happen...*

'There,' he said. 'As good as new.'

'Thank you,' Cat said, pulling herself together with an effort. 'But that's more than can be said for those jeans—or your handkerchief.' She regarded the glistening muddy streaks on both items with disfavour. 'You'd better have them laundered and send me the bill.'

'You pay for your clothes,' he reminded her. 'I pay for my own laundry. But it was a kind thought.'

'Yes—well.' She offered him a swift, meaningless smile. 'I'll—see you later.'

'You can count on it.' He paused. 'But I think we've forgotten something. I don't know your name. You don't know mine.'

'Is it strictly necessary?' she asked with spurious brightness. 'After all—ships that pass in the night and all that.' She shrugged. 'It might even be—more exciting not to know.'

'Well, we all have our own separate ideas of excitement,' he said with a touch of dryness. 'But I'd still like to know what you're called.'

'Then it's Catherine,' she said reluctantly. 'But I'm always known as Cat.'

His brows lifted. 'Not Cathy—or Kate?'

'Absolutely not. It's because of the story.' She shrugged again. 'Someone once told me I was like *The Cat That Walked By Itself.*'

'I wonder if that's true.' He looked back at her, half frowning. 'I suppose you have a surname as well?'

'And I'm sure you do too,' she said evenly. 'But we're not going to use them—and that's my part of the deal. First names only.'

He said slowly, 'Very well. If that's how you want it.' He paused. 'And I'm Liam. Sometimes known as Lee, but only to my intimates. So I'm afraid you don't qualify.'

'I'll try and get over the disappointment. Besides, I'd probably be lost in the crowd anyway,' Cat told him coolly. 'And now I'd better get back to the killing fields.' She hesitated. 'So where do you want us to meet—this evening?'

'Don't worry about that.' His faint smile did not reach his eyes. 'When the time comes—I'll find you.'

And he turned and walked away, leaving Cat staring after him, her face expressionless but a thousand alarm bells ringing in her brain.

CHAPTER TWO

I MUST be losing my grip, Cat thought grimly as she made her way back to the hotel, trying not to hurry too obviously in case he was watching from somewhere. *Because this is a serious overreaction on my part.*

It was ludicrous to feel like this—as if she was helpless, or threatened in some way. Because that was far from the case. She, Cat Adamson, was quite capable of taking care of herself.

And, yes, Liam—or Lee-to-his-intimates—was undeniably loaded with attraction, but he was by no means irresistible. In her scheme of things no man was.

No doubt he'd sampled all the local talent and decided to spread his net a little wider. A born opportunist, she told herself scathingly, who would benefit from the set-down she was planning to administer. Not that he was likely to see it that way, of course. But she doubted it would do any real harm to the male arrogance flourishing under all that dangerous charm.

What was it he'd said? *I guess I'll have to settle for what I can get—for now, at least...*

What was that supposed to mean? she wondered. Not that she was ever going to find out, because, whatever she might have said, she wasn't keeping this date.

Instead, she would simply cancel the room she'd booked for the night and be back in London before he even knew she was gone. And that would draw a final line under an episode which had disturbed her far more than she wanted to admit.

At the terrace steps she hesitated, taking a quick look back over her shoulder. But he was nowhere to be seen, she realised with a quick sigh of relief. Probably his tea-break, or whatever, was over, and he'd decided to return to work. She could only hope he wasn't operating anywhere near the car park.

She stepped back into the Banqueting Suite, and straight into a wall of noise. The music had begun and people were dancing, their faces flushed and grinning, their buttonholes and corsages wilting in the heat.

Cat found her hand seized by the best man, Freddie's recently divorced older brother. 'I've been looking for you all over the place.' He smiled at her winningly, eagerly. 'Come and dance.'

She complied, because there was no real reason not to, even though she suspected she was going to find herself the target of some pretty determined flirting. His wife had left him for her boss, and Tony was clearly anxious to re-establish his own pulling power as a result.

He was obviously still raw over Cheryl's defection, so Cat humoured him, at the same time gently deflecting his efforts to discover her London address and phone number. In spite of his bravado, he wasn't really looking for a casual relationship, she thought. He already had the house, the job and the car, and he needed a wife to complete the set. And, as he was better-looking than Freddie, and an altogether nicer character, she was sure he would succeed. Only not with her.

She found, disturbingly, that Liam's image kept swimming back into her consciousness. That she was focusing almost greedily on the memory of his smile—his touch. And that the mere thought of them was making her senses tingle and her mouth go dry. Well—that could stop, right here and now, she told herself with grim resolution.

Gritting her teeth, she threw herself into the fray of the party. She loved to dance, and there were men queuing up to partner her. There were lots of people who wanted to chat, too—old friends and neighbours of her aunt and uncle, who remembered her from childhood and were glad to see her again.

But that also had its trying side. 'Haven't you brought a

young man?' they kept saying. And, even worse, 'It'll be your turn next.'

Over my dead body, Cat thought, smiling until her jaw ached, while she fervently agreed that Belinda and Freddie, who were dancing together stiffly, with fixed smiles, made a lovely couple.

It was a distinct relief when the pair of them disappeared, amid applause, to change into their respective going-away outfits.

And as soon as they'd left for their honeymoon, Cat decided, she would also be on her way. All she had to do now was get out of this dress, which she would happily never see again, put on the casual skirt and top she'd arrived in that morning, repack her overnight case and pay her bill. She would undoubtedly be charged for her cancelled night's booking, she thought, with a mental shrug, but it would be worth it for a speedy getaway.

But as she began to edge round the room she was pounced on by her father, looking furious.

'Would you kindly have a word with your mother?' He started in without preamble. 'Request her to show a modicum of civility to my future wife?'

'No,' Cat told him with sudden terseness, glaring back at him. 'I will not. I'm tired of being the messenger in this stupid war you're waging on each other. From now on the pair of you can do your own dirty work.'

Good God, she thought. I can hardly believe I said that. I usually sigh, and agree to do my best.

Her father sent her a look that combined shock with sorrow. 'I'm disappointed in you, Cathy,' he told her heavily. 'But then, you've always taken your mother's side against me.'

'Not,' Cat returned drily, 'according to my mother. Actually, I've done my damnedest to remain impartial, but that clearly hasn't worked, so I'm going to become uninvolved instead. If you have bullets to fire, use your own guns.'

She met his measuring glance calmly. Then David

Adamson's face relaxed into a rueful, charming grin. 'Point taken. But can I at least offer you a lift back to town when this is over?' He lowered his voice confidentially. 'I'd really like you and Sharine to become friends.'

Cat wondered cynically if the other girl would be around that long, but she kept her doubts to herself.

She said merely, 'Thanks, Dad, but I've brought my own car. Another time, perhaps.'

He winced. 'Call me David, please, my darling.' He made an expansive gesture. 'Dad is so—so...'

'Ageing?' Cat suggested. 'I'll try and remember. Especially in front of Sharine,' she added drily.

She set off again, skirting chattering groups, calling greetings with a smile, but finding herself, inevitably, detained by others. Having to talk and be civil in spite of the pounding urgency to be gone that was building inside her.

And when she finally reached the door her mother was waiting for her impatiently. 'What was your father saying to you?' she demanded. 'Was he talking about me? And is he really planning to marry that—bimbette?'

'I suggest you ask him yourself,' Cat said coolly. 'As I told him, I've decided to abandon my role as go-between once and for all.'

Vanessa's brows rose incredulously. 'Heavens, sweetie, you sound almost militant. What's prompted this? Too much champagne?'

'I drank half a glass for the toasts,' Cat returned.

'Hmm.' Vanessa pursed her lips. 'Then perhaps you need more.'

'Maybe I need my parents to start behaving like adults.' Cat glanced round her. 'Where's Gil?'

'Oh, he's met someone else who's a photographer. They're discussing cameras somewhere,' Vanessa said vaguely. She brightened. 'I'm going to be in London for at least a week. Why don't we all have dinner together? It's time you got to know him. We're staying at the Savoy.'

Cat hesitated. 'That would be—good. But I'm pretty tied up at work just now.'

'Well, I'm sure you can make some time for me—if you try.' Vanessa sent her a glittering smile. 'And I might have some work for you myself. A friend of mine wants to revamp her entire Knightsbridge house, and I told her how brilliant you were. She's dying to hear from you.'

'Mother,' Cat said patiently, 'I've told you—I don't do houses. We're commercial designers. Find a friend with an office block and I'll be happy to help.'

Vanessa pouted. 'It's not very glamorous. And I have so many contacts—I know I could get you all kinds of commissions. You could earn a fortune.'

'I'm doing fine, thanks. And you and Dad cornered the glamour market a long time ago.' Cat gave her mother's scented cheek a quick kiss. 'You look terrific, by the way.' She forced a smile. 'Gil must be doing something right.'

'Oh, he's an angel,' Vanessa said, almost absently. 'But what about you, sweetie? Clearly you're here on your own. Isn't there someone you could have brought?'

Cat shrugged. 'I didn't look. Besides, I prefer to keep my weekends free.'

'It does seem such a waste. And half my friends are grandmothers.' There was an oddly wistful note in her mother's voice.

Cat's brows lifted. 'In one of your recent interviews,' she pointed out mildly, 'you implied that I was still at school, and certainly below the age of consent. You can't have it both ways.'

'No.' Vanessa paused, her smile almost wry. 'I'm beginning to realise that.'

There was a sudden stir in the hotel foyer, and the guests began to surge towards the door of the Banqueting Suite. Cat found herself carried along with them.

Belinda was coming down the stairs, pretty in a pale blue dress and jacket, followed by a plainly sheepish Freddie. She paused theatrically, holding up her bouquet amid laughter and cheering, then tossed it high into the air. Cat realised it was coming straight for her and took a hasty side-step, clasping both hands behind her back for good measure.

Out of the corner of her eye she saw a hand reach up and grab it by the streamers of its white silk bow. There was a moment of stunned silence, then the cheers began again with a sudden roar.

Looking round, Cat saw with real shock that it was Vanessa who was standing, smiling as she held the flowers clasped in front of her. Saw her mother turn to Gil, who'd materialised at her side, reaching up to pull him down triumphantly to her kiss.

And saw, too, her father, standing a few yards away, as if he'd been turned to stone. His face was like a mask, but it was the expression in his eyes that stunned her. There was a blaze of anger there, but there was pain too, stark and ocean-deep.

Cat took one horrified step towards him, then paused as Sharine got there first, sliding her arm through his as she pressed her body seductively against him. She murmured something that made him look down at her, his mouth relaxing into a smile.

Perhaps it had just been a trick of the light, Cat thought, turning abruptly away. But the moment was over, whatever it had meant.

She went back into the suite, deserted now but for one solitary figure sitting at a table, her fingers pulling at the spray of roses she was wearing, systematically destroying it petal by petal.

Cat said uncertainly, 'Aunt Susan—they're just leaving—Belinda and Freddie. Don't you want to say goodbye?'

Her aunt shook her head. She said quietly, 'I seem to have been saying that for a long time now.' She paused. 'Some things end—others begin. That's the way it works—isn't it?'

Cat knelt beside her impulsively. 'Would you like me to come back with you tonight? Stay for a day or two?'

Susan Adamson stroked her cheek almost absently. 'No, my dear, but thank you for offering. I have a lot of thinking to do, and I need to be alone for that.' She paused, forcing a smile. 'I may even go away myself for a while. I need a rest after all this—chaos.' She gestured around her at the littered tables, but Cat knew she wasn't merely referring to the wedding.

'I'll be in touch,' she promised quietly.

With the departure of the bridal couple a sense of anti-climax had set in, and people were already beginning to drift away. As Cat went towards the stairs she glimpsed her uncle in a shadowy corner of the foyer, talking with soft urgency on his mobile phone.

No prizes for guessing who he was calling, she thought, remembering bitterly her aunt's quiet, contained expression.

Even now people were stopping her. 'So good to see you again, Catherine.'

'Thank you.' She couldn't even try any more to match names to faces.

'What a marvellous day it's been. Gone without a hitch.'

'Yes, fantastic.'

'So lucky with the weather.'

'Perfect.'

Were they all blind? she wondered incredulously as she finally won free and went upstairs to her room. Hadn't they realised what was going on in front of them? Or were they too carried away by vintage champagne and their preconceptions of married bliss to care?

And what would they have done if she'd stood up and shouted the truth aloud?

Ignored me, probably, she decided with a wry twist of her mouth.

But everything that had happened simply confirmed and

hardened her resolution to stay clear of entanglements—especially the emotional kind.

They're not worth the suffering, she told herself.

Sighing, she unlocked the door of her room and went in. The deep sunlight of early evening was pouring through the window, bathing the pastel walls and the charming flower-sprigged fabrics in a mellow glow.

Cat found herself sending the wide, canopied bed a regretful glance as she discarded her wedding finery and put it into her case, after extracting clean underwear and a plain white skirt, to be teamed with a short-sleeved knitted top in dark blue silk. She'd been looking forward to spending the night here and waking to the sound of birdsong instead of London traffic.

She examined her sandals minutely before packing them, but apart from a tiny fleck of mud on the inside of the heel, which she removed with her thumbnail, they were as good as new. Apart, of course, from the memories they evoked. She wouldn't rid herself of them quite so easily.

On the whole, rural peace offered rather too many opportunities for brooding, she decided, particularly over things that she could not change.

For an uncomfortable moment she found herself remembering the way her mother had spoken of grandchildren, and David's immediate reaction when Vanessa had caught the wedding bouquet and smiled up into her lover's face.

But they were actors, she reminded herself with sudden harshness. So who could say if the emotions she had glimpsed were genuine?

Apart from that, the Anscote Manor Eden had its own built-in snake, she thought, her mouth twisting. So it would be far more sensible to get back to the city, real life and sanity, and avoid unnecessary temptation. Because this Liam was simply not for her—and for all kinds of reasons.

She bit her lip. She was still ashamed of her unguarded

response to his touch. And for all the other emotions he'd made churn inside her.

He knew exactly what he was doing, she thought bitterly, as she reached for the phone to call Reception. And I allowed it. Even though I am not—repeat *not*—into one-night stands.

'This is Miss Adamson in Room Ten,' she said briskly, when her call was answered. 'I've decided not to stay the night after all, and I'd like my bill to be made up, please.' She glanced at her watch. 'I'll be leaving in about three quarters of an hour.'

She went into the bathroom, cleaned off every speck of make-up, then took a leisurely shower, letting the warm water stream over her.

Washing away, she hoped, the residue of the day. And any lingering resonances there might be.

She towelled herself down, applied some of the lily-scented skin moisturiser she'd found in the array of toiletries provided, then, wrapping herself sarong-like in a fresh towel, she wandered back into the bedroom.

Collecting the hairdryer, she seated herself on the broad cushioned seat under the window while she finger-dried her hair into its usual sleek shape. The view below was of formal gardens, with gravelled paths bordered by teeming summer flowers.

The local Lothario seemed to know a lot about his job, too, she thought with an inward grimace, her eyes straying half-unconsciously to the golden gleam of the lake in the distance. He'd certainly created the perfect romantic backdrop for a little intimate adventuring.

So it would do him good to find himself ditched and left high and dry.

And it would make her feel better too, knowing that her moment of weakness had passed and she was back in control again.

She dressed, added a touch of blusher to her face and a

hint of lustre to her mouth, slid her feet into low-heeled navy pumps, then collected her bag and jacket and went downstairs.

The place seemed deserted, she thought, looking around her. Everyone had disappeared, off in their different directions, and Belinda's wedding was well and truly over at last.

There was no one at the desk either, so she rang the small silver bell. After a minute a girl in a dark suit emerged from the inner office, looking harassed.

She checked when she saw Cat. 'Oh,' she said. 'Are you the lady from Room Ten who wants her bill?'

Cat's brows lifted. 'Yes,' she acknowledged. 'Is there some problem?'

The girl's colour deepened. 'We're having problems with the computer. It's a new system, and it's swallowed some of our data. We've got an engineer coming, of course, but we can't make your bill up just yet.' She moved her hands awkwardly. 'I—I'm very sorry.'

Not half as sorry as I am, Cat thought, glancing at her watch with inner dismay. Time was passing rapidly and she needed to be gone.

'Don't you have some kind of back-up?' she asked. 'Or couldn't you just calculate what I owe you with a paper and pencil? Anything?'

'I'm afraid not, but I hope we won't have to keep you too long. The engineer is on his way.' The girl hesitated, looking uncomfortable. 'Would you like to wait in the lounge?' she suggested. 'Or the bar, maybe?'

'No,' Cat said. 'I think I'll go back to my room.' She paused. 'And if anyone enquires, will you tell them I've checked out and gone, please?'

The receptionist looked wary. 'Yes,' she said slowly. 'I suppose we can.'

Well, don't knock yourself out, Cat thought, torn between annoyance and amusement.

'And can you send up a tray?' she requested. 'Just coffee

and some sandwiches. A selection of what's available would be fine,' she added, with a shrug.

'Certainly, Miss Adamson.' The girl spoke more confidently. 'I'll see to that right away.'

This has not been my luckiest day, Cat told herself ruefully, as she let herself back into her room.

She found the paperback novel she'd brought to read in bed, and curled up with it on the window seat, trying to relax. It was going to be a glorious sunset, she thought, promising more fine weather tomorrow. She might go out somewhere— to Kew, perhaps, or on the river.

She returned her attention to the book, but found it difficult to focus. She felt too edgy—too restless to give it the concentration it deserved.

She got up and walked round the room, eyeing the telephone and wondering if Reception would have the wit to tell her once the computer was working again.

She kicked off her shoes and lay across the bed on her stomach, her chin propped on one hand while she flicked the remote control through the TV channels with the other. But there was little to engage the attention there either, so it was almost a relief when a tap on the door announced the belated arrival of her coffee and sandwiches.

She called 'Come in,' and as the door opened added, 'Put the tray on the table by the window, please.'

Liam said, 'I cancelled the food order. I was afraid you'd spoil your appetite for dinner.'

Cat heard herself yelp. The remote control skittered out of her hand to the floor as she flung herself upright, her eyes blazing.

She said, breathlessly, 'What the *hell* are you doing here?'

'I just told you.' He sounded mildly surprised. 'I came to explain about the food.'

'Damn the food,' she said tautly. 'You're the gardener, for God's sake. So who gives you the licence to roam into guest bedrooms with any kind of message?'

He propped himself against the dressing table. 'I don't confine myself to the great outdoors.' He had the gall to sound faintly amused. 'My talents are many and varied.'

Even though she was furiously angry, it occurred to her, as she stared haughtily back at him, that if he hadn't spoken she might not have recognised him. The scruffy jeans and shirt, she saw with growing amazement, had gone, and been replaced by a pair of elegantly cut charcoal pants. His crisp white shirt, open at the neck and with the cuffs turned back over his forearms, accentuated his tan.

The dark hair was neatly combed, and he'd clearly shaved. She could breathe the tang of some expensive citrus cologne in the air.

He'd gone from extremely attractive to seriously glamorous in one stride, she thought, swallowing.

She, on the other hand, was desperately at a disadvantage, barefoot, flushed and dishevelled, kneeling in the centre of a large bed.

All this, she thought, is really bad news.

He sent her a mocking grin, as if he'd guessed the tenor of her thoughts. 'Do you still want to wait until eight o clock?' he queried softly. 'Or are you hungry now?'

She took a deep breath. 'Look,' she began, 'it was kind of you to offer me a meal, but I really have to get back to London tonight. I'm just waiting for the computer to produce my bill.'

'Well, it's not ready yet,' he said. 'So you may as well eat—with me.'

'I think,' Cat said, keeping her voice steady, 'that you're going to have to learn to take no for an answer. Starting now. So, will you please leave my room?'

He settled himself more comfortably against the dressing table, making her disquietingly aware of the lean strength of his body. And that he had the air of a man prepared to wait, as well.

'Tell me something,' he invited. 'What are you so afraid of?'

'Oh, that's an old ploy,' Cat said scornfully. 'I'd have expected better of you.'

Liam shook his head. 'It's a positive request for information. You had a room booked for the night, yet you were so keen to run out on me that you asked the receptionist to lie for you. Why?'

'I had second thoughts,' she said curtly. 'And I considered you might be troublesome about them.' She lifted her chin. 'I certainly got that right, didn't I?'

'What in hell,' he said slowly, 'do you imagine I'm going to do to you?'

'Now you're being ridiculous,' Cat said, ignoring the fact that the imagination in question was currently running riot. Her stomach was churning in turmoil and her mouth was dry.

He said, 'You seem—uneasy, that's all. A trifle—on edge.'

'Nonsense,' she said, too quickly. 'As I said, I have—stuff waiting for me in London. I decided I should make a start on it—that's all.'

'Even if it meant breaking a promise?' His eyes met hers. Held them.

'It wasn't a firm arrangement.' Cat bit her lip, aware that her breathing had quickened. 'I—I didn't think you could be serious—or that you'd believe that I was.'

He nodded thoughtfully. 'Because I'm merely part of the hired help and you're a lady from London with appointments to keep and deals to be made?'

'No,' she said. 'Because you're a complete stranger, and it didn't seem—appropriate.'

'Yet that's how things begin,' he said. 'With strangers meeting. And, according to statistics, a lot of those strangers actually meet at weddings too.'

'We didn't exactly do that—if you remember.'

'I have total recall,' he said. 'Of every detail. You're The Cat That Walks By Herself, and all places are alike to you. Isn't that how it goes?'

Her brows lifted. 'Bravo.'

'But if that's really the case,' he went on, as if she hadn't spoken, 'there's nothing to prevent you being with me for a while. Going my way for a change.' He smiled at her. 'After all, what have you got to lose?'

More, she thought, *than I even want to contemplate...*

She said tautly, 'Are you always this persistent?'

'Are you always this elusive?'

'It doesn't occur to you that I might—just prefer my own company?'

'How can you know,' he said, 'until you've tried mine?' He gave her a considering look. 'Of course, if you're too ashamed to be seen with me in the restaurant, we could always dine up here.'

'No!' The denial seemed to burst out of her.

He grinned at her. 'No to the shame, or no to being alone with me?'

She lifted her chin. 'Both.'

'What's the matter, Cat?' His voice was soft—goading. 'Discovered some hot bricks? You'll feel better when you've eaten.'

She was silent, knowing that she'd run out of arguments yet hating to admit it. 'Very well,' she conceded reluctantly, at last. 'If—if I must.'

'You overwhelm me,' he murmured. He allowed his gaze to wander over her for a meditative moment. 'Tell me something—is that bed as comfortable as it looks?'

Cat stiffened defensively, angrily conscious that she'd started to blush. 'It's all right. Why?'

'Because you seem to be glued to it.' He unhitched himself from the dressing table and came towards her. 'Need a hand?'

From somewhere she managed a steely glance. 'No, I do not. Thank you.' She paused. 'I—I'll join you downstairs.'

'Will you, now?' He was grinning again, she saw with chagrin. 'I think it might be safer if I waited for you right outside—just in case you have some alternative getaway planned. And don't be too long,' he added softly. 'Because I seem to be developing quite an appetite.'

And he left her kneeling there, in that absurd ocean of sprigged bedspread, staring after him, her heart thudding unevenly and her arms wrapped round her body like a shield.

CHAPTER THREE

You don't have to do this, Cat told herself as she ran the cold water tap over her wrists in an effort to calm her juddering pulses. You could simply call up the manager and tell him that a member of his staff is annoying you—something you should have done hours ago. He'll then be removed, and probably fired. Following that, you proceed on your way.

Always supposing Liam decided to go quietly, she amended unwillingly, which was by no means certain. After all, she had agreed to have dinner with him, and she could hardly deny that without telling a downright lie. And lying—even childish fibs—had always made her thoroughly uncomfortable.

And if, as well, it meant him getting the sack...

I don't want him on my conscience, she thought with an inward grimace. Just out of my life.

But then she didn't want him smiling at her across the dinner table either. Her stomach gave an odd little lurch at the idea. And exactly what colour were his eyes, anyway—grey or green? And how did he manage that trick of laughing with them when the rest of his face was completely straight?

Don't even go there, she advised herself tersely, as she retrieved the compressed powder from her cosmetic purse and attempted to tone down the flaring colour in her cheeks.

Maybe the best idea was just to have dinner with him. To treat him with faintly amused indifference, as a passing irritation to be dealt with and then discarded. A matter of no importance. Three courses and no coffee before she made her excuses and finally headed back to London. Alone.

She certainly didn't want him to think he had got to her in any way, so she would have to play it cool.

She ran a comb through her hair, straightened her skirt, then walked with pretended composure to the door.

She paused, drawing a deep breath. Let the game begin, she instructed herself silently, then turned the handle.

Liam was leaning against the wall opposite, but he straightened instantly when he saw her, a lightning glance sweeping her from head to toe.

'There's really no need to be nervous,' he mentioned softly as he fell into step beside her. 'After all, everyone has to eat.'

'I'm not nervous,' Cat snapped. 'Simply annoyed at your— unwarranted persistence.'

His slow grin was unperturbed. 'Oh, you were out of sorts long before I showed up. You've had a trying day. What you need is some rest and recreation.'

She stared straight ahead of her. 'I already had that planned—at home.'

'Where, of course, you live alone.'

'Yes,' she acknowledged curtly. 'If it's any concern of yours.'

'Naturally I'm interested,' he drawled. 'Or I wouldn't be here now.'

Fool, she castigated herself silently. You should have claimed you lived with a boyfriend—or shared a house with three other girls. The last thing you need is to sound vulnerable—or available.

But the truth was she didn't seem able to think straight. Merely walking down this wide staircase beside him was taking a strange kind of toll on her. He wasn't touching her— there was actual space between them—but all the same she was trembling inside, her senses tuned to a kind of scared anticipation she had never experienced before.

And just when she needed to be most in control, Cat thought, biting her lip.

They were clearly expected in the dining room, where the head waiter conducted them to a corner table in an alcove without a flicker of surprise. And even, she realised, puzzled, with a modicum of deference.

They must consider he can pay the bill, and that's what matters, she thought with a mental shrug as menus were brought, napkins spread, the inevitable candles lit and aperitifs offered. Which she swiftly declined, asking for mineral water only.

'Very circumspect.' Liam's lips twisted as he ordered a whisky for himself.

'I'm driving,' she said. 'Or had you forgotten?'

'Not at all. But I still think it's a pity you changed your mind about staying the night,' he added meditatively.

Why does that not surprise me? Cat thought, sheltering behind her menu.

'Is that what's known as a dignified silence?' her infuriating companion enquired, after a pause.

'On the contrary,' she returned. 'I was merely trying to choose between the melon and the chilled cucumber soup.'

'And have you reached a decision?'

'The soup,' she said. 'And grilled Dover sole, please. Off the bone.'

'Make that two.' Liam turned to the hovering waiter. 'But I'll start with the goat's cheese tartlet.' He picked up the wine list and indicated his choice.

'Not steak?' Cat asked when they were alone, raising her brows in faint mockery. 'I had you down as a red meat man.'

Liam took a reflective sip of his whisky. 'Any other assumptions about me that you'd like to share?'

'Well…' Cat considered. 'You're certainly a risk-taker.'

He leaned back in his chair. 'Based on what?'

She shrugged. 'Pestering a female guest to spend the evening with you. I'm sure that isn't part of your job description.' She tried another steely glance. 'How did you know I wouldn't make a formal complaint about you to the management?'

'Because you're Cat,' he said softly. 'And all cats are curious.'

'That's it?' she queried scornfully. 'You staked your future here on some old saying?'

He grinned at her. 'Not just one. How about "Faint heart ne'er won a lady fair"?'

'You have not,' she said, '*won* me.'

His grin widened into provocation. 'Perhaps I haven't been trying.'

It was an open challenge, and she knew it. She'd had plenty of time to absorb her surroundings and realise that theirs was the most secluded table in the restaurant, practically screened from the rest of the diners. The candlelight, too, seemed to enclose them in this private microcosm. And although she could hear the murmur of voices and the chink of glassware and cutlery from the rest of the room, Cat still felt cut off. Isolated. With him.

She said coolly, 'You have an inflated idea of your own charm.'

'I'm sure your powers of resistance are equal to it.' Liam paused as the wine waiter arrived at the table with an ice bucket and a bottle of white burgundy. He tasted it, then nodded, and the waiter turned to Cat, filling her glass before she had a chance to refuse.

As the man departed Liam lifted his glass. 'A toast,' he said quietly, his eyes meeting hers. Lingering enigmatically. 'To the promise of the evening.'

Cat felt her skin warming involuntarily under his gaze. She bit her lip, raising her own glass in turn with open reluctance. It was certainly not the toast of her choice, she thought broodingly.

She hadn't planned to drink any alcohol, either, but had to concede that it was a wonderful wine, filling her senses with its cool, seductive fragrance.

Under other circumstances, she thought, with something approaching regret, this could indeed have been an evening to remember. As it was...

She lifted her chin. 'Not just a risk-taker,' she commented with faint derision chilling her voice. 'But an optimist, too.'

'Everyone is allowed to have their dreams.' He was still watching her. 'What do you dream about, Cat?'

'Oh, I never remember,' she said untruthfully. 'Anyway, I think I'm too busy to dream.'

'Really?' His brows lifted. 'So, what keeps you so occupied?'

Studiedly, she put down her glass. Gave him a brief, composed smile. 'Sorry,' she said. 'No more personal details.'

'Won't that tend to make conversation tricky?'

'Not my problem.' She shrugged. 'After all, I didn't choose to be here tonight. Which means I reserve the right to protect my privacy. No other options available.'

'But hardly the ideal way to start a relationship.'

'We're having dinner,' she said. 'Nothing more than that.'

He was leaning back in his chair, his face half hidden in the shadows beyond the candlelight. 'To you, perhaps,' he said. 'But not to me. It will take a damned sight more than a meal to satisfy me tonight.'

She bit back a gasp. She said huskily, 'How—dare you? Are you mad?'

'No,' he said. 'I'm a risk-taker—and an optimist. You said so yourself.' She could hear the sensuous huskiness in his voice. Could feel the smoky intensity of his gaze on the roundness of her breasts under the clinging top as acutely as if he'd touched them naked, cupping the warm swell of them in his hands.

She felt suddenly breathless, the pounding of her heart like a trip-hammer, as she found herself imagining how his touch would be...

Oh, God, she thought, retreating from the brink. This cannot be happening. Pull yourself together.

Now, if ever, was the time to tell him with flinty emphasis

that he'd finally overstepped the mark, pick up her bag and leave—even if it meant leaving the hotel a blank cheque for her bill.

Only, she realised, dismayed, the first course was arriving and their table was surrounded. Bread was being offered, butter pats placed within reach, and glasses were being topped up. An exit was no longer a simple option—if her legs would even carry her so far.

Instead, as if she'd been programmed, she found herself picking up her spoon and addressing her soup. Its cool, delicate flavour was just what she needed to ease the dryness in her throat. And maybe food would stop the trembling inside her—if anything could…

'Good?' Liam asked casually, host to guest rather than predator to prey, and she nodded jerkily.

'Wonderful,' she managed. 'The food critics seem to be absolutely right.'

'I'll make sure I tell the chef.'

'Yes, please do.' Cat reached for the nearest glass, intending to drink some water, only to find she'd taken another gulp of wine.

But if she confined herself to one glassful only there'd be no real harm done, she assured herself hastily. Perhaps it would even calm her a little—help her to relax and endure the remainder of the meal.

Because that was what it was going to be—an endurance test. And she had to be the winner. There could be no other result.

So perhaps it was time she tried to recover a measure of control over the situation.

She took another deliberate sip of wine, then smiled at him with direct charm. 'What a good idea this was,' she said. 'Thank you.'

'My God,' he said mockingly. 'And I thought you were all set to sprinkle hemlock on my salad.'

It was an effort, but Cat retained the smile. 'On the contrary. I'm always excited to try out new restaurants.'

'I was sure you would be,' he said gravely. 'Although eating in can be fun, too.'

'Possibly,' she said. 'In the right company.'

His mouth slanted in wry acknowledgement. 'Do you like cooking?'

'That's another personal detail,' she said. 'Therefore taboo.'

He considered this for a moment. 'Don't you find the maintenance of your defensive shield a little wearing?'

'Not at all.'

'Ah,' he said. 'Then may I find it tedious on your behalf?'

The swift bubble of laughter escaped her before she knew it.

She tried to regain lost ground by glancing at her watch. 'Well, tedium won't last for much longer. I have to be on the road within the hour.'

His hand reached across the table and took hers, keeping it in a light clasp, his thumb stroking the slender bare fingers.

He said quietly, 'Don't go. Stay here tonight.'

In an instant the whole atmosphere had changed—become electric. Cat felt her throat tighten as she heard the deafening throb of her own blood. Felt the heat begin to build inside her.

She shook her head, not trusting her voice, her entire body awakening to his light, sensuous touch. It shocked her to know how much she'd wanted to say yes—to abandon herself to whatever the night might bring. She was bewildered and almost frightened by this strange turmoil in her senses.

She looked down almost wonderingly at the hand still holding hers, and stiffened slightly, a faint crease appearing between her brows. His fingers, she saw, were long and lean, and very strong for all their gentleness.

But, she realised, they were also smooth, and without calluses, and his nails were immaculately clean and neatly trimmed.

She said shakily, pulling her hand from his grasp, 'You're not a gardener at all, are you? Or any other kind of manual worker?'

His voice was quiet. 'I never said I was.'

'No, but you let me think so.' Cat paused, vexed, as the waiters returned to clear the plates and serve the next course. She drank some wine, the stem of her glass gripped tensely, as she watched them bone the fish and place the fillets on to plates. A bowl of tossed green salad was set on the table, with a dish of tartar sauce, and a platter of tiny sauté potatoes was offered.

All of which gave her a chance to think—to regroup and regain her composure. But also prompted her to start wondering about him all over again.

She'd already noted, of course, that his change of clothes was expensive, but there were few other clues. He wore a watch on a plain black leather strap, and no rings, which could mean anything or nothing.

When they were alone again, and had begun to eat, she said, striving for lightness, 'It seems I really must stop jumping to conclusions.' She paused. 'So, if you're not the gardener, what's your real connection with this place?'

Liam tutted reprovingly. 'You're breaking your own rule, sweetheart. The embargo on personal details works both ways.'

Cat stared expressionlessly down at her plate. Caught, she told herself, without humour, in my own trap. Why didn't I see that coming?

Because he's knocked you sideways, said a small mocking voice in her head. And you're not thinking properly. He's awoken all your senses except common sense.

She forced a smile. 'Maybe I should rethink my position.'

'On the contrary.' His answering grin was totally relaxed. 'I'm starting to enjoy this enforced anonymity.' He began to count off on his fingers. 'No searching for common ground. No discovery of mutual friends or wincing over tastes in books and music. No mobile phone numbers or e-mail addresses.' He paused, adding softly, 'No past and no future. Simply—the pleasure of the present.'

Which is exactly what I spent most of the afternoon telling myself I wanted, Cat thought startled. So I can hardly complain now that it's here.

She said crisply, 'Pleasure is something of an exaggeration.'

'Ah,' Liam said gently. 'But the night is still young.' His eyes met hers, then moved down slowly to absorb the quiver of her parted lips.

She drank some more wine, her mind whirling again. There'd been hunger in his gaze, and purpose too, and her body had warmed under the overt suggestion.

Oh, God, she thought, what am I getting into? Am I actually contemplating making love with someone I didn't know existed when I woke up this morning? Am I seriously that crazy?

Because it was one thing to declare her own sexual independence in the mid-afternoon under a blazing June sun, and quite another to go from theory to reality by plunging into intimacy with a stranger in the warm shadows of the night.

That would be a huge—maybe an irrevocable step for her. And she wasn't sure whether she had the courage—or the sheer bravado—to take it.

She lifted her chin. 'Why, yes,' she said lightly. 'And there could even be chocolate for dessert.'

'I can guarantee it,' he said. He paused. 'And after dessert?'

Cat tensed. 'What do you mean?' She tried not to sound breathless, but wasn't convinced she'd succeeded.

'I thought—coffee,' he said. 'And armagnac, perhaps? After all, I suspect you're already over the driving limit.'

She looked at her empty wine glass—at the upturned bottle in the ice bucket. So much, she thought, for good intentions.

'Yes,' she said. 'I—I suppose I am.' She swallowed. 'Well—that sounds—good.'

The chocolate torte, when it came, was good too—sublimely rich and totally delicious—and she ate every crumb, her concentration on the food masking the fact that her mind was churning.

There were things about him she really needed to know, she told herself as the coffee and brandies arrived. And first and foremost among those was his marital status. After all, he already knew she was single. She wanted the same assurance about him.

He might be sending her body wild, but there was no room in her life or ethos for other women's bored husbands.

And there was no way of finding out except by direct questioning, which, as she'd already seen, would get her nowhere.

'I'd give a year's pay,' he said quietly, 'to know what you were thinking.'

She glanced up, smiling wryly. 'I imagine that could be quite a sacrifice.'

Liam took a sip of brandy. 'Another fishing expedition?'

'Not at all.' She gave him a composed look. 'I was thinking that we've both absorbed a certain amount of information about each other already. For instance I know that you like uncomplicated food—beautifully cooked—and that you like to play games,' she added.

'That,' he said, 'seems to be something we share.' He paused. 'And I know, of course, that you're not a big fan of weddings. Tell me—was bloodshed actually avoided at today's affair?'

'Fortunately, yes.' *If you discount the internal bleeding,* Cat thought, wincing. 'But it was still fairly grisly,' she added lightly.

'Was that why you decided to change your clothes? A kind of ritual cleansing?'

She shrugged evasively, lifting a nervous hand to the neckline of her top. She said, 'I needed something more comfortable to travel in, that's all.'

'Yet you haven't been comfortable at all.' His voice was gentle. 'You're still very much on edge—aren't you?'

Cat bit her lip. She knew that he was right—that she'd been restless throughout the meal, her fingers pushing back her hair from her face, playing with the gold bracelet of her watch, or constantly raising her napkin to her lips.

He, on the other hand, the cause of her unease, seemed supremely relaxed, long legs stretched out in front of him, while she sat with her feet tucked primly back under her chair, making sure there was no contact.

'Perhaps,' she said. 'It's been a hell of a day, but I—I didn't realise it had affected me that much.'

'Treat it as a learning curve.' His long fingers were playing casually with the stem of his glass. She watched their movement from under her lashes, as if mesmerised, just as she'd covertly studied his every gesture, each turn of his body throughout the meal. Intensely aware of him, she realised, all the time. Unable to break free. Drawn ever more deeply into his web with every second that passed.

He gave her a faint smile. 'Decide here and now that your own wedding day will be completely different. Totally angst-free.'

Cat poured herself some more coffee, thankful that she could keep the cafetière steady. 'Actually, I've been far more decisive than that.' She sent him a cool smile. 'Because I'm planning not to have a wedding at all—ever.'

There was a silence. Liam looked at her, his brows lifted. 'Isn't that a little radical?'

She shrugged again. 'I have it filed under "necessity". As far as I'm concerned, the whole concept is outdated—and totally surplus to my requirements.' She paused. 'You disagree?'

'I can't say I've ever given it a great deal of thought.' He leaned back in his chair, his face meditative. 'And I've certainly never been tempted to try it,' he added. 'If that's what you wanted to know in some convoluted way.'

He allowed that to sink in before continuing, 'And isn't this conversation straying back into the forbidden zone?'

'Perhaps.' Cat met his gaze squarely—full eye contact. 'So, having yielded a point, do I get to know what you're thinking too?'

There was a silence, then he said quietly, 'Are you sure that you want to? You might not like the answer.'

'It's seems only fair,' she said. 'So I'll take the risk.'

'Then I have to confess that I'm indulging all the basic male fantasies.' His eyes went to her mouth, then travelled down to the swell of her breasts. His tone was clipped, his mouth unsmiling. 'I'm remembering that moment this afternoon when I held you, and felt you tremble against me. I'm imagining what it would be like to have you in my arms again, and to kiss you—and how you'd look without your clothes.'

She felt as if all the air had been sucked out of her lungs. She was shaking again, but not from shock—or fear. Her heartbeat quickened almost painfully.

From some great distance she heard herself say quietly, huskily, 'How strange, because I'm wondering much the same about you.'

Liam pushed back his chair and rose. He came round the table to her, taking her hand, pulling her to her feet.

He said softly, 'So why waste any more time? Why don't we simply go upstairs—and satisfy our mutual curiosity?'

He looked deeply into her eyes. 'Well?' he asked, and she nodded mutely in reply.

Still holding her hand, Liam strode through the restaurant, threading his way between the tables.

Cat tried to hang back. She said breathlessly, 'But we can't just leave. There's the bill to pay...'

'They'll know how to find me,' he said. 'When they need to.'

They climbed the stairs together, side by side. When they reached the door of her room Cat said, 'Will you give me a few minutes?'

He framed her face in his hands, looking down at her, his mouth wry. 'Having second thoughts, Cat? Planning to run away again—or lock your door against me?'

She shook her head. 'None of those, I—I promise. I just—need a little time to myself.'

'Maybe we both do.' He released her, his hand stroking the hair back from her face. 'But don't keep me waiting too long.' And strode away.

The room, she discovered, had been made ready for the night—curtains drawn, bed turned down, the lamp lit on the night table and her nightgown fanned across the coverlet.

The hotel staff must have known all along that she would stay, Cat thought, biting her lip. Just as she had known it herself, of course, in spite of her denials.

She undressed without haste and put on her nightgown, adjusting the narrow straps on her shoulders. She brushed her hair, and sprayed her pulse-points with her favourite scent.

Then she turned off the lamp and drew back the curtains, opening the window a little so that the cool fragrance of the night drifted into the room along with the moonlight.

As she turned back into the room she caught a glimpse of herself in the mirror. In her filmy gown, with its low-cut bodice and straight skirt, she looked like a slender ghost. But the swift hammer of her pulses and the heat invading her body told her that she was all too mortal.

His knock at the door was quiet.

'Come in.' Her voice was equally subdued, even shaking a little.

He had changed too, she saw. He was barefoot, and she knew that his dark blue silk dressing gown was his only covering.

He stood watching her for a long moment, the open hunger in his gaze mixed with a kind of wonder that made the breath catch in her throat.

He said huskily, 'You are almost—too beautiful. Do you know that? So lovely that you scare me.'

She shook her head, colour sweeping into her face. She felt shy, suddenly, and incredibly vulnerable in the face of his passion.

She tried to smile. 'I'm frightened too—a little.'

He came slowly across to her, resting his hands lightly on her bare shoulders, his thumbs stroking the delicate hollows of her collarbone.

He said, 'But I'm not the first? I can't be.'

'No.' Cat, for one strange moment, found herself wishing desperately that her answer could have been different. That she could have told him she was still a virgin—that there had been no other man in her life and that the night ahead with him would be her true initiation.

She said, 'Liam...'

'Shh,' he whispered. 'The past doesn't matter. Just the pleasure of the present—remember?'

He bent his head and found her mouth with his. Her lips parted willingly, eagerly under the questing pressure, meeting the sensuous invasion of his tongue with her own ardent warmth.

His fingers slid down her arms to her waist, then moved to the base of her spine, his hands hard as he drew her against him and the heated passion of his arousal, and Cat sighed brokenly as she felt her body respond to his desire with its own surge of liquid fire.

When the long kiss finally ended, she was trembling like a leaf caught in the wind, her breathing shallow and driven, astonished at the depth of emotion he had engendered in her.

She took one small step backwards, away from him, staring at him with enormous eyes as slowly she hooked her fingers under the thin shoulder-straps and pulled them away and down, releasing herself from her nightgown.

As it slipped to the floor the delicate fabric seemed to shiver against her fervid flesh, grazing the hardening peaks of her expectant breasts, lingering for the length of an indrawn breath over her hips, until she faced him, naked, her body an exquisite challenge.

Her voice was a husky wisp, half lost in the depth of the silence between them. 'Now it's your turn.'

Liam made a small harsh sound in his throat. He untied the belt of his robe and shrugged it away, then lifted her in his arms and carried her to the waiting bed.

He lay beside her, his lips on her mouth, her throat, as he caressed her breasts with gentle, awed fingertips. She arched towards him, yielding and sinuous, her hands beginning an exploration of their own, stroking his muscular shoulders, then moving slowly down his spine to the flat male buttocks.

He had, she thought, a wonderful body—lean, tanned and smooth-skinned, apart from a shadowing of body hair on his chest. Cat buried her face in his shoulder, absorbing the scent of his skin, marvelling how familiar and precious his nakedness seemed.

Only a few hours ago they'd been strangers, she thought wonderingly. Now, in this moonlit bed, they were becoming lovers, intimate and enthralled.

He muttered hoarsely, 'Hold me,' and she obeyed, her fingers encircling the taut velvet hardness of him, paying delicate tribute to his potent masculine strength.

Sighing with pleasure, Liam lowered his mouth to her breasts, his tongue adoring the engorged nipples until she moaned aloud with the pain and glory of it, aching for his possession, and felt him smile against her skin as he whispered, 'Wait, my love.'

He moved slightly, turning away from her, and she murmured his name in disappointment and appeal, only to realise he was simply taking care of her by using protection.

He came back to her, framing her face with his hands, kissing her deeply and sensually. Then his fingers were parting her thighs, exploring the sweet, scalding heat of her, his touch light, but almost agonisingly precise. Now gossamer, now fire.

And at the moment when the sheer agony of her need was threatening to overwhelm her Liam slid his hands under her hips, raising her slightly to receive him in one powerful thrust.

She responded instantly, fiercely, her hands gripping his shoulders, her legs lifting to enfold him and draw him even closer.

He moved rhythmically and without hurry, sinking his body deeply into hers. Taking her with him quite inexorably, it seemed, to some distant place. Somewhere she had glimpsed so many times, but arrived at so rarely.

This time, she told herself. This time...

She heard his breathing change, the pace of his movements quicken, and knew that, for him, the moment was there. But that once again it had passed, leaving her behind. So when his body shuddered its way into the ultimate rapture, and he flung back his head, calling her name, she cried out too, her panting voice rapturous.

She pulled him down to her, clasping him as he groaned out his release, her mouth seeking his with unassuaged hunger. When it was over for him he lay very still, eyes closed, his body slick with sweat.

At first she thought he was going to sleep, and that was something she was also accustomed to. But to her surprise he moved, lifting himself away from her. Clearly he did not plan to sleep in her arms, and the realisation gave her an odd pang.

For a few long moments there was only silence, and Cat lay motionless, not wanting to disturb him.

Then she felt him stir, and the next moment his hand reached out, gently but firmly taking her chin and turning her to face him. He was lying, propped up on one elbow, apparently replete and relaxed. He was smiling faintly, but his eyes were narrowed slightly as he regarded her.

'So,' he said quietly, 'how was it for you?'

'Wonderful,' she said, and smiled back into his eyes. 'Surely you don't need to ask?'

He said slowly, 'If it was that great, why didn't you come?'

She swallowed. 'But I did...'

'No,' he said. 'I'm not a fool, Cat, and I know you were pretending. You were with me almost to the last moment—I could feel it—and then I lost you somehow. You seemed to—drift away.'

There was a silence, then Cat released herself from his clasp, biting her lip. 'I—I'm sorry.'

'You have nothing to apologise for.' His tone was dry. 'Obviously I should have taken more time—been more considerate.'

She didn't look at him. 'I don't think that would have made much difference. It just—doesn't happen for me very often.'

'Yet you wanted me,' he said gently. 'You weren't faking that.'

'I can't explain it,' she said in a muffled voice. 'It's as if I reach—and reach—but there's nothing there.'

'And is it like that every time?'

To which the answer was, Pretty much, Cat thought. But she had no intention of saying it.

'I don't think that's up for discussion,' she said. 'After all, we agreed—no past, no future, just the pleasure of the present.' She paused. 'Or are you some kind of psychotherapist, wanting to delve into my subconscious? Because I'm not buying.'

'No,' Liam said, a sudden harshness in his voice. 'I'm the man who's just failed to satisfy you. But at least I can do something about that.'

He pulled her to him, stifling with his mouth any protest she might have planned. But at the first touch of his lips Cat was beyond resistance, her surrender absolute.

His hands were travelling slowly down her pliant body, lingering, arousing. Making every sense, every nerve-ending quiver in this new awakening. And where his hands touched his mouth followed, feathering kisses on her vulnerable flesh.

His tongue teased her breasts, turning the rosy peaks to tingling hardness, and she closed her eyes, sighing, conscious of nothing but the piercing delight of the sensations he was evoking.

When he raised his head, she heard herself say thickly, 'Don't stop—you can't stop...'

'I've only just begun.' There was a shadow of laughter in his answering whisper.

His lips travelled on down, over the flat plane of her stomach, caressing the tiny whorls of her navel, the hollows of her hipbones. His hands were stroking her thighs, and her body slackened in anticipation of the contact she yearned for, but which, tantalisingly, he did not seem to be offering.

'Please.' Her voice did not seem to belong to her. 'Oh—please.'

Then she cried out as his mouth reached the joining of her thighs and found the molten, aching sweetness within. For one shocked, bewildered moment she tried to push him away, scared of this depth of intimacy, but he captured her wrists with one hand and held her helpless.

His tongue was a flame, gentle but intense, as it began to explore her most secret being, seeking her small hidden bud and coaxing it to exquisite life. He made it flicker against her, then stroke her with delicate finesse, before circling on her with voluptuous control. And without mercy.

Cat was breathless, small sounds coming from her throat as her head twisted on the pillow. There were tiny golden stars dancing behind her eyelids, and she could hear the blood roaring through her veins like the echo of a remorseless tide beating on the shore.

Everything else—each sense, each nerve, each atom of emotion—was focused, concentrated on this passionate agony of sensation he was creating for her. Nothing else existed but this lesson in her own sensuality that she was being taught by a master. She wasn't even aware of the moment when he released her wrists.

Her inner heat was raging like a furnace. She realised in some outreach of her mind that she had reached the brink and was being held there endlessly, her body a silent scream for release.

When it came, it was like a quiet pulse beating deeply and insistently within her, gathering power and strength, rising to some undreamed-of height. Until he took her across the edge, and her body imploded into rapture, shuddering violently as each tremor tore through her.

And his name on her lips was a thanksgiving.

CHAPTER FOUR

AFTERWARDS, Cat lay, held close in his arms, absorbing the small ripples of delight that still assailed her, like the aftershock of an earthquake, with tears running down her face.

'My darling,' Liam said softly, kissing her wet eyes. 'My clever angel. Don't cry.'

Her voice trembled. 'I never knew it could be like that—never dreamed...'

'I knew,' he told her gently. 'From the first moment that we looked at each other, I knew.'

She sighed. 'Maybe I'm not as sophisticated as I thought.'

'So I discovered.' There was a wry twist to his mouth as he stroked her cheek. 'Along with the fact that Cat the Tigress does not take her claws to bed. You're quite an enigma, my love.'

'Is that better than being a male fantasy?' she queried sleepily, her head tucked into the curve of his shoulder.

A laugh shook him. 'Just different.' He added softly, 'But I think you'll still be fulfilling my fantasies long after I've solved the mystery.'

She barely heard him. She was already drifting, heavy-lidded, into sleep. Sinking down through waves of contentment into a haven of dreamless rest.

When she awoke it was daylight, and fitful sunshine was glancing into the room through the open curtains. And she was alone in the big bed, with the covers drawn neatly over her.

What was more, she was once again wearing the nightgown she'd discarded a few hours previously, she realised, touching the soft fabric with disbelieving hands.

As she sat up and looked round the room Cat experienced

54

a curious sense of disorientation. Because there was simply
no sign that the room had ever been occupied by anyone but
herself. Even the pillow beside her was plumped up and pristine.

Had the events of last night simply been a figment of her
imagination? A kind of wish fulfilment? Could she have only
dreamed Liam, and the rapture she'd found with him?

No, she thought, her body quickening with excitement.
That wasn't possible. Her senses were still basking in the
afterglow of his lovemaking.

And her last memory was breathing the scent of his skin
as she lay with her head on his shoulder and her face turned
towards the curve of his neck.

Broodingly, Cat drew her knees up to her chin, her mouth
tightening.

Falling asleep in his arms had not been part of the plan—
if, of course, she'd ever had a plan. Somewhere along the
way she'd been hijacked, all her good intentions blown to the
four winds.

But sharing her bed for an entire night had always seemed
to her to be a dangerous step towards sharing her life. There
was an ocean of trust implied in abandoning one's consciousness in the presence of another person, and it was something
she'd always avoided in the past, offering some light and
credible excuse—she had an early start in the morning, or she
was a poor and restless sleeper. Anything that would send
them on their way and re-establish her privacy, her inviola-
bility.

On the other hand, how did she know he'd spent the night
with her? After all, she had no idea when he'd decided to
leave, not when she'd been so dead to the world that he'd
been able to dress her in her nightgown without waking her,
for heaven's sake.

She bit her lip hard. It seemed ridiculous to jib at that when
there was not one inch of her body that he had not caressed
and kissed with such passionate skill and artistry. When she'd

not just accepted all the intimacies of their lovemaking but gloried in them. Yet somehow having her gown replaced when she was asleep and helpless seemed a familiarity too far.

However, it seemed unlikely she would ever be able to take him to task about it, she told herself. Because he was probably no more committed to the idea of a relationship than she was herself. And maybe the way he'd erased all signs of his presence was his version of goodbye, avoiding all excuses or explanations.

She'd set herself up, she thought with sudden bleakness, for a one-night stand. So she could hardly complain that Liam had taken advantage of that—and of her. Or that he'd walked away afterwards.

Cat bent forward, resting her forehead defeatedly on her knees and squeezing her eyes so tightly shut that they hurt. At the same time she was aware that no physical pain could even compete with the small, bewildered ache deep within her. Or the inexplicable sense of loss.

A sudden rap at the door had her shooting upright, her whole body tense, her mouth dry.

'Who—who is it?' she managed.

'Room service, madam.' A woman's voice. 'Your breakfast.'

A key rattled in the lock and she came in, middle-aged, brisk and efficient in a striped overall, carrying a tray. Swiftly she unfolded its supporting legs and placed the tray across Cat's lap.

Cat, bewildered, was confronted by fresh orange juice, warm croissants in a basket, with dishes of honey and black cherry jam, and a tall pot of coffee. And a single red rose in a narrow crystal vase.

She hadn't ordered any food, but maybe breakfast came with the room—and she couldn't deny that she was hungry, she thought, as she thanked the woman with a smile and unfolded her napkin. Besides, she had the journey back to

London ahead of her, and she had no wish to undertake it on an empty stomach.

Although there was nothing she could do about the strange void which seemed to have opened up inside her where her heart should be.

Don't even think like that, she adjured herself with sudden fierceness. It's irrelevant. You're not looking for a soulmate but a lover, for the occasional night of mutual passion and fulfilment, and in that respect Liam could have been the answer to your prayer.

But he's gone, so you'll just have to forget the 'might-have-been' and continue the search elsewhere—one of these days.

And, with a determined nod, Cat applied herself to her breakfast.

The meal over, she repacked her case, leaving out only a change of underwear and the clothes she'd worn the previous evening, then went into the bathroom to have a shower.

She stood for a while, eyes closed, under the powerful cascade, relishing its sting against her flesh, then reached for the soap.

But someone was there before her.

'Allow me,' Liam murmured, sliding warm arms around her and drawing her back against him.

Cat yelped, her heart banging against her ribcage in shock. 'What are you doing here?' she demanded raggedly as she started to breathe again.

'I came to wish you good morning,' he said, deftly taking the soap from her unresisting hand and making it into a lather. He began to apply it slowly and gently to her damp skin, making little circular movements, covering her breasts, belly and thighs with the creamy foam.

Cat felt an almost drugging weakness begin to invade her senses under his ministrations, and realised that if he hadn't been holding her she would probably have slid limply to the floor of the shower.

'But I'm not going to ask if you slept well, because I know you did,' he added softly in her ear.

'Yes.' It was barely more than a croak. Her head fell back against his shoulder as the delicate movements of his hands shifted to a more intimate dimension.

'But now...' his lips found the sensitive spot beneath her ear '...now you're awake again.'

Her only answer was a sigh, as Liam discarded the soap and began to caress her breasts, teasing the excited nipples with his fingertips. She could feel the pressure of his arousal, and moved against him with deliberate provocation.

His reaction was immediate. He turned her to face him, his mouth seeking hers hotly and without reserve, then lifted her in his arms and brought her down to him, his wet, slippery body joining effortlessly with hers in one swift act of possession.

Cat clung to him, mouth locked to his, her arms round his neck and her legs twined round his waist, her whole self attuned to the burning rhythm of his powerful thrusting. Her own response was ardent and complete.

When the first tiny tendrils of pleasure began to uncurl inside her she gasped against his lips, but as the sensations intensified, and she felt all control sliding away, she gave a small, frightened cry.

'Don't fight me, darling.' He muttered the words hoarsely into her mouth. 'Just—let go.'

The breath sobbed in her throat as she obeyed, and felt the first fierce shaft of ecstasy piercing her to the soul. She could hear herself moaning in a kind of delirium as her body seemed to dissolve in one rapturous convulsion after another, and was aware of him shuddering against her as his body found its own powerful release.

She was still clinging to him, sated, exhausted, when he turned off the water and lifted her out of the cubicle. He grabbed a bath sheet from the rail and flung it round them both as he carried her into the bedroom.

When she could speak, she said, with a kind of wonder, 'Is that—really how you say good morning?'

They were lying on the bed together, still wrapped in towelling, as well as each other's arms.

Liam kissed her gently on the mouth. 'Indeed it is,' he murmured. 'Also goodnight, and on really lucky days good afternoon, too.'

'My God,' she said faintly. She moved back a little, studying him. 'How did you get in here, anyway?'

'The chambermaid left the door open for a moment when she came for your tray.'

'How—extremely fortunate.'

'Indeed,' he said gravely. 'I must remember to leave her a generous tip.'

'I thought you'd—simply gone.' Now, why had she said that? Cat wondered with vexation. It sounded really needy. And that was the last impression she wanted to convey.

'No,' he said. 'That was never part of the plan. As you should know by now. I merely thought it would be more discreet if I had breakfast in the restaurant, that's all.'

'Yes,' Cat said. 'Of course.' She began to disentangle the bath sheet, and his hand shot out and captured her wrist.

'Hey, where are you going?'

'I have to get dressed,' she said. *Because it's far too beguiling, lying in your arms like this. I could get to enjoy it far too much, and I can't afford to do that. It's too dangerous.* 'Besides,' she added quickly, 'this towel is getting clammy, and the chambermaid could come back.'

'The door is locked,' he said. 'And I hung the "Do Not Disturb" sign outside.'

'You were very sure of your welcome.' She introduced an austere note.

He grinned at her. 'Not at all. Just—hopeful.'

'But we can't stay here,' she said. 'There's a check-out time.'

'And you have to get back to London.' He sighed. 'If you

insist on putting your clothes on, could you walk round the room without them a couple of times? I want to check if my photographic memory still works.'

It was ludicrous, after what had happened between them, but Cat felt herself blushing.

She made her voice sound light as she reached for her clothing. 'I think we both have enough memories to be going on with.'

'Spoilsport.' Liam lay back, watching her, his head pillowed on his folded arms. 'I'm going back to London too,' he said, after a pause. 'Which makes it convenient.'

'In what way?' Cat zipped herself into her skirt.

'In that I won't have to travel from one end of Britain to the other when I pick you up for dinner tonight,' he returned.

There was a long silence. Cat's hands fumbled on the button of her waistband, then reached for her top and dragged it over her head.

Liam studied her, brows slightly raised. 'You don't object to that, I hope?'

She said slowly, 'You don't know where I live.'

'But I'm relying on you to tell me,' he said. 'Address, telephone, fax, e-mail, date of birth, favourite flower—every last detail that you wouldn't tell me last night.'

She touched dry lips with the tip of her tongue. 'I—I don't think I want to do that.'

Liam threw off his share of the towel and stretched indolently, making her sharply aware of every lean, suntanned inch of him. 'Then I shall have to rely on my powers of persuasion.' He held out his hand, his smile wickedly enticing, making the breath catch in her throat. 'Come here, darling—please.' His voice was husky.

She felt her pulses begin to race. Experienced the first stirrings of that delicious melting sensation all over again.

Realised how much she wanted to do as he asked—how desperately she ached to go to him and allow herself to be drawn down into his arms.

Into his arms and into the trap, she reminded herself with sudden force. Lured there by the possibility—the dream of a shared future.

Forgetting how starkly the past twenty-four hours had demonstrated how the dream could turn to nightmare. The harsh evidence from her own family circle.

You begin as strangers, she thought, then you allow yourself to be seduced—confused by passion into believing that this time it will be different—eternal. But when passion dies you're strangers again, with all the hurt and bitterness that implies. And the loneliness.

The image of Aunt Susan sitting alone, a silent statue amongst the post-wedding clutter, came into her mind. And for some reason that odd expression on her father's face as he watched her mother catch Belinda's bouquet. Even Belinda, putting a brave face on the humiliation she'd suffered on what was supposed to be her great day.

'Cat?' Liam was sitting up, his brows drawn together in a frown. 'Cat—what is it? You look as if you've seen a ghost.'

'Do I?' She moistened her lips with the tip of her tongue. 'Liam—there's something I have to say.'

His frown deepened. 'My sweet, if you're about to tell me that you're married after all, then you've chosen a seriously bad moment.'

'No,' she said. 'No, of course I'm not married. I told you yesterday that doesn't feature in my plans—now or ever.'

'Yes,' he said. 'We both talked a lot of nonsense yesterday. But that was then. Last night changed everything. It had to. You must know that too.'

'Perhaps,' she said. 'But not in the way you think.' She paused. 'What are your plans for the rest of the day—as a matter of interest?'

'Nothing very extraordinary.' The grey-green eyes were suddenly searching. 'We both have our own cars, so I thought on the way back to London we could meet up in Richmond. There's a good place to eat by the river.'

'And afterwards?'

Liam shrugged. 'We could go for a walk in the park. Talk to each other. Start getting properly acquainted. Unless, of course, you have a better suggestion?' he added levelly.

'Maybe not better.' She shrugged. 'Just—different.'

There was a silence, then Liam swung himself off the bed. 'You got dressed to have this conversation,' he said quietly. 'I'm starting to think I should do the same.'

He walked over to the chair where his discarded clothes were piled and began to pull them on. It didn't take long. He faced her in faded khaki pants, which closely hugged his lean hips and long legs, and a black V-necked sweater in thin wool, his bare feet thrust into loafers.

He said, unsmilingly, 'So—what's on your mind?'

Her whole body clenched in yearning as she looked at him. She swallowed.

'I need you to know that everything that's happened between us has been—wonderful,' she began. 'Last night was unbelievable—the most exciting of my entire life.'

Liam leaned a shoulder against the wall. 'Thank you,' he said. His eyes were guarded—watchful. 'I think. For what it's worth, I found it totally amazing too. And unforgettable.' He paused. 'But if you're now about to tell me that this—brief encounter of ours is all there is to it,' he went on grimly, 'that you've decided for some reason to lock me out of Paradise, then I have to warn you, lady, that you've got a fight on your hands.'

'No,' she said. 'That's not what I mean at all. More than anything I want to go on seeing you.'

'I'd like to feel encouraged by that,' he said slowly. 'But somehow I can't. I wonder why?'

Cat decided to ignore that. She said, 'Do you want to know why I found our time together so exciting?'

'I thought it might be because we clearly wanted each other so desperately,' he said. He shrugged a shoulder. 'But what do I know?'

'And because it was so unexpected,' she said eagerly. 'So—overwhelming. We met—we made love.'

'I don't recall it being quite that simple,' Liam said drily. 'But go on.'

'One of the things that made it special was that we knew so little about each other. We weren't bogged down in a lot of extraneous detail. We both knew what we wanted, and we went for it. It added an extra dimension—a kind of danger. Because we were free.' She paused, giving his expressionless face an anxious look. 'You must have felt that too.'

'I think I was probably too sexually enthralled to dwell much on the philosophical ramifications,' Liam drawled. 'It's a man thing. But I'm still listening.'

Cat was shaking inside suddenly, but she threw her head back with an assumption of confidence. 'I don't want to lose that excitement—that edge.'

'You feel that could happen? You're threatened by the prospect of lunch in Richmond?' His smile did not reach his eyes.

'Yes,' she said. 'I think it's a risk if we get involved in things like that. In walks and talks and theatre trips. In meeting each other's friends and all the usual banal stuff.'

'I don't consider my friends banal,' he said. 'I can't, of course, speak for yours, but I'd have thought it unlikely.'

Cat gestured impatiently. 'That was just an illustration.' She paused. 'But do you see what I'm getting at?'

'I'm not sure,' Liam said slowly. 'At least, I hope I'm not. Maybe you should be more specific.'

She took a very deep breath. 'I want to go on seeing you. I want us to be lovers, just as we've been here. Meeting on completely neutral territory. Not asking any questions or imposing any obligations. Just—enjoying each other.'

He turned and looked out of the window. He was very still, but Cat could sense the tension in him like a coiled spring.

'And then parting?'

'Well, yes,' she admitted lamely. 'Until the next time.'

'So,' he said. 'That's all you want from me? Sex in a series of hotel rooms just like this? Paid for by the hour?'

'No,' Cat denied swiftly. 'It's far more than that. Something completely separate from our everyday selves, and infinitely special. A private affair with a secret lover. Knowing each other's names, but nothing else. Passion without commitment.' She paused, wishing she didn't have to speak to his taut back. 'Doesn't that turn you on just a little?'

Liam swung round, and Cat gasped and fell back, confronted by the blaze of anger in his eyes.

'Frankly, no.' His voice bit. 'I think you must be out of your mind even to suggest it.'

'Why?' she flared in turn. 'Because the idea's coming from me—the female of the species—and setting up a discreet liaison is a male preserve? Isn't that just a tad hypocritical?'

Two long strides brought him to her. His hands gripped her arms, the fingers digging into her flesh. His face looked stark, stripped to the bone. 'You try to set me up as your tame stud and you expect me to be bloody pleased? What the hell do you think I am?'

She tried to pull away. 'Liam—you're hurting me...'

'Hurting you?' he said, his voice shaking. 'My God, I'd like to—'

He stopped, biting his lip savagely, then released her with a contemptuous gesture, turning away from her again.

When he spoke again his voice was cool and even. 'And when passion fades—what then?'

She hesitated. 'Then we finish it, quietly and sensibly, like adult people.'

'Ah, yes,' he said. 'Rather like putting down a wounded animal.' He paused, looking back at her, his eyes hooded. 'Tell me something—how many other men have been offered this enticing proposition, just as a matter of interest?'

She looked down at the carpet. 'None,' she denied quietly. 'I—I thought I'd found the perfect lover at last—and I wanted to go on seeing you.'

'But only in secret,' Liam said with icy scorn. 'And on your terms, at designated locations and specific times. Two anonymous bodies joining, then separating. Contact without contact. How incredibly romantic.'

Cat lifted her chin. 'You can't bear it because I've been honest with you,' she accused. 'Because I've made it clear I don't want to get involved in a full-blown relationship. If the situation was reversed no doubt it would be perfectly acceptable. But because I refuse to be trotted out as the official girlfriend when you need someone to take to a party,' she added heatedly, 'or I balk at cooking meals for you at the weekends and taking your clothes to the dry cleaners, then I suddenly become a Grade A tart.'

'I took you to bed, sweetheart,' he said harshly. 'That does not make you an authority on my domestic arrangements or necessarily a candidate for any kind of commitment on my part, whatever you may wish to think. You're way ahead of yourself there.'

'It was you,' she said, 'who mentioned lunch and a stroll in Richmond Park.'

'That was my mistake.' His tone grated across her skin. 'It won't be repeated.' He walked across the room to the door, where he paused, looking back at her.

'"The Cat that walks by herself",' he quoted with icy mockery. 'I should have taken that nonsense more seriously.'

'Liam.' Her voice trembled, and she could taste the salt of tears in her throat. Tears that she refused to shed. 'Don't leave like this—please. Let's talk about it. Let me make you understand. You see—I—I want you.'

'That's unfortunate,' he said. 'Because you can't have me.' He shook his head. 'I just hope that you don't find it too lonely out there, sweetheart—while you're searching for my replacement.'

And the door closed behind him.

Cat stood rigidly, staring in front of her, her hands clenched at her sides.

CHAPTER FIVE

'I CAN'T let him go like this. I can't...' Cat whispered, as finally she shook free of her trance-like state and forced herself to move. She ran to the door and flung it open, but the corridor outside was empty. All the other doors were inimically shut.

Slowly, she retired back into her own room and sat down on the edge of the bed, wrapping her arms round her body in a gesture of bewildered self-protection as she struggled to master her breathing.

She could hardly believe his uncompromising reaction to her plan. She'd expected initial incredulity—even to be laughed at—and probably an argument. But not the kind of anger that flayed the skin from her bones. Nor had she anticipated that he'd walk out on her with such finality.

And if I had caught up with him? she thought. What could I have said? That I was sorry? That it was all a joke and I didn't mean it? Because it wouldn't be true.

She had wanted to be honest with him. Had needed to make him understand the limitations of any relationship between them.

But Liam hadn't wanted the secret, passionate affair she'd offered. In fact it wasn't certain that he'd been in the market for an affair at all, she thought, feeling her face warm as she recalled his scathing comment. Maybe, as he'd told her, she'd taken far too much for granted, and his only intention had been a brief sexual interlude to enliven a dreary weekend in the country.

After which it would have been thanks and goodbye.

Which hardly justified him seizing the moral high ground,

66

but some men seemed adept at taking the double standard in their stride, and perhaps he was one of them.

Except that she didn't really believe it, Cat told herself in sudden fierce negation. Whatever he might have said or done.

He wanted me, she thought. I know he did. But not enough to accept my terms. But I can't offer more. I dare not. Not to him, or anyone.

Dear God, I've only known him for a few hours, and I already feel as if the heart's being ripped out of my body. How could I possibly allow him closer, to become a real part of my life, when I'm halfway to falling in love with him already? And, however absurd that may be, I simply can't risk it.

In a way, Belinda's wedding had been a catalyst, showing her clearly the sorrow and disillusion that could await those who loved and trusted, turning into iron her determination to go her own way.

A cloud of unhappiness and disaffection had hung over the whole event, she thought, and now, in spite of herself, she'd been caught in it too.

A long, shuddering sigh escaped her.

Love's a game, she thought. A game where the rules change every minute. And my life's in place, so I have no room for that. I can't afford it.

But if we'd spent the rest of the day and the night together, as Liam wanted, I might never have been able to let him go. And I knew that. I recognised the temptation. Saw the danger I was in. I had to try and regain control over the situation—and myself.

And in doing so I lost him.

She bent her head, hugging herself closer still as she acknowledged the pain of that and tried to deal with it. She could smell the soap he'd used on her skin. Was aware of the faint tenderness between her thighs from the fierce rapture they'd shared. Felt her throat tightening, and the harsh prickle of tears at the back of her eyes.

How could things change so suddenly? she asked herself, almost despairingly. Only fifteen minutes ago she'd been lying happily in his arms, her body glowing from his lovemaking. Everything to play for. Now he was out of her life for good, and she was left stunned and shocked at her sense of desolation.

The room, she thought, shivering, still seemed to carry echoes of his anger. It would be a long time before she forgot the contempt in his eyes, or his scornful words as he walked away from her.

But then it would be an even longer time before she'd be able to erase anything about Liam from her mind, she realised unhappily. When she closed her eyes he was there, as if he'd been somehow etched into the lids of her eyes.

One thing was certain. She would not be searching for anyone to take his place, as he'd so harshly suggested. She had been taught a harsh lesson, and she needed to gather her resources. Rethink her strategy.

One day, far in the future, someone might cross her path who also wanted a no-strings affair.

But he would not be Liam, she thought, and one tear trickled scaldingly down the curve of her cheek.

She stared down at her feet. The pale pink polish on her toes matched the colour on her fingernails, unflawed, without the slightest chip. Ironic, she thought, to look so groomed and orderly on the outside and be falling apart inside.

She drew a harsh breath, then jumped determinedly to her feet. This kind of emotional turmoil was exactly what she wanted to avoid, and the room itself did nothing for her mood.

Instead of sitting here, moping, she should take positive action.

She picked up the damp bath sheet and folded it, then replaced it in the bathroom and collected her bag of toiletries, dropping her soap into the wastebin.

Time for a change there, she told herself, biting her lip as she made a last check that she'd packed everything.

Her last action was to glance in the mirror, making sure that she didn't look as wrecked as she felt. Her mouth was still slightly swollen from Liam's kisses, and there were weary shadows beneath her eyes, but she'd pass, she told herself.

There was a different receptionist today. Cat placed her key on the desk. 'I hope the computer's recovered,' she said briskly. 'Because I'd like my bill, please.'

'The computer?' The girl gave her a puzzled look. 'Has there been something wrong? No one's mentioned it to me.'

'Then it must be all right again.' Cat produced her platinum card, and stood waiting as the receptionist busied herself at the screen.

She could always enquire about Liam, she thought, touching the tip of her tongue to dry lips. Forget her own rules and find out who he was. Keep it casual, keep it feasible. A magazine he'd lent her, perhaps, which she wanted to return.

For a moment she found herself regretting the absence of one of those old-fashioned hotel registers, the kind that people used to sign along with their personal details, and private detectives used to consult on the sly when the receptionist's back was turned. It was all done with cards these days, which was no help at all—least of all to private detectives.

But what good would it do? she asked herself ironically. She'd be far better off taking a solemn vow to stop beating herself over the head like this.

The receptionist turned back to her, looking even more bewildered. 'I'm sorry, Miss Adamson, your bill has already been settled.'

'No,' Cat said firmly. 'That can't be. I tried to pay last night, but the computer was down. I told you.'

'But I assure you it has been paid—in full.' The girl ran off a copy of the statement and handed it to her. 'See?' She was smiling brightly. 'You don't owe us a thing.'

'And you don't understand,' Cat returned. 'I haven't paid it.'

'Well.' The smile faltered for a moment, then redoubled its

efforts. 'Maybe someone's treated you to it. After all, you were here with yesterday's wedding party.'

'Yes,' Cat agreed slowly. 'That must be it.'

She was nearly at the door when the girl called to her. 'Miss Adamson, I've just found this note in your pigeonhole. It must have been left while I was on my break.'

Hotel stationery, Cat thought as she took it. And her name in one angry slash on the envelope.

Woodenly, she tore it open and extracted the single sheet.

The message was brief. 'I don't usually pay for sex,' it read. 'But last night was exceptional.' And Liam's initial.

She restrained an impulse to crumple it into a ball in her hand, or tear it, screaming, into a million pieces.

'Are you all right, Miss Adamson? You look very pale. Not bad news, I hope.'

Cat started, and began to hastily reassemble the rags of her composure. 'No,' she said. 'No, not at all,' she said, thrusting the note into her bag.

You need to leave with your head high, she told herself. And you can do it. You have to.

She looked back at the receptionist, whose smile must surely be making her mouth ache by this time.

'I'm fine.' Her voice was clear and strong. 'And thank you—for everything.'

And she walked out into the sunshine, to her waiting car.

Cat was thankful to find herself back in the office on Monday morning.

All things considered, it had been a hell of a weekend, and it would be good to put her personal problems on hold and deal with issues she had some chance of solving.

She had driven back to London without even stopping for lunch—in Richmond or anywhere else. Traffic had been heavy for a Sunday, and by the time she'd reached her flat she'd had a splitting headache, not improved by finding imperious messages from both her parents on her answer-machine, demanding she contact them without delay.

Later, Cat had thought, pressing the 'delete' button. When I'm feeling stronger.

She'd taken a couple of painkillers, then undressed and had a bath, washing herself from head to foot with almost minute care. When she was dry again she had got into the ancient velour robe which was her equivalent of a comfort blanket then she moulded some kitchen foil into a container and burned Liam's note, washing the ashes down the sink.

One lot of memories dealt with, she had told herself. Although the remainder might not be so easily erased.

She had found a can of vegetable soup in one of the kitchen cupboards, and some cold chicken in the fridge, and put together a scratch meal which she'd eaten doggedly, without any pretence at enjoyment.

After that she had gone to bed, falling almost immediately into a heavy but restless sleep, fragmented by brief, disturbing dreams.

'Still hung over?' Andrew, her boss, enquired, brows lifted in amusement when she arrived for the morning conference. 'Must have been a good wedding.'

She smiled back calmly. 'We don't do things by halves in our family.'

It was a typical Monday, with decorators going sick, solemn promises on delivery dates for furniture and fittings blithely abandoned, and recently ordered fabrics and carpets suddenly becoming discontinued.

Cat spent most of the day alternately arguing and cajoling with workmen and suppliers on the phone and by e-mail.

But her tender to redesign the workspace in an elderly office block on the edge of the City had been successful, and there was a string of enquiries from potential clients to be fielded too.

By the end of the day she felt sufficiently ahead of the game to return her parents' calls.

'So lovely to have seen you, darling,' Vanessa purred. 'Let's get together, shall we, for a lovely long chat—girlfriend stuff?'

That indicated that Gil would not be present, which was one blessing, Cat thought wryly. She said, 'I had the impression we were mother and daughter.'

'Don't get technical, my sweet.' Vanessa's tone was waspish. 'Gil says there's no way I look old enough to have a grown-up daughter.' She paused. 'Shall we say Wednesday evening at eight—my treat?'

Cat sighed silently, but agreed. Presumably the idea of becoming a grandmother had lost its popularity, she thought as she put the phone down. But that, too, was all to the good, she told herself defiantly, fighting the sudden rawness in the pit of her stomach.

'You seemed a little out of sorts on Saturday,' was her father's greeting.

'It was hardly the event of the year,' Cat pointed out drily.

'No.' David paused. 'There's been a development,' he added heavily. 'It seems your uncle has moved out of the house and gone to live with his secretary.'

'Oh, God.' Cat felt slightly sick. 'Poor Aunt Susan.'

'He must be out of his mind,' said her father shortly. 'Ditching an incredible woman like that.'

'You feel you have any place to criticise?' Cat asked, her voice hardening.

'There's no comparison between the two situations,' he defended. 'Your mother's temperament was a nightmare. For heaven's sake, girl, you were there.' His tone was injured. 'You saw what went on.'

'Yes,' Cat said curtly. 'I also know it was a long time ago, and maybe you should stop apportioning blame and move on.' She hesitated. 'Have you talked to Aunt Susan?'

'Briefly,' he said. 'To be candid, I found it a little awkward. She didn't say a great deal, although I did offer to go down there, of course.'

'Did you plan to take Sharine with you, by any chance?' Cat played restively with a pen on her desk.

'Well, naturally. I can hardly leave her in London by herself.' He paused. 'I gather from your silence that you think it's a bad idea?'

'I've seen the secretary,' Cat mentioned drily. 'Another young blonde.'

'Ah,' David said quietly. 'I see. In that case, this could be something you might tackle.'

'And I think she might need time and space to deal with it, initially,' Cat said. 'Without being inundated by her husband's relations, however well-meaning.'

'That's rather harsh,' he protested. 'I've always been devoted to Susan, and she knows it.'

'Of course,' Cat returned. 'And you should think well of her. After all, she brought up your only daughter.'

There was another longer silence, then he said grimly, 'Thank you for reminding me, Cathy,' and put the phone down.

Cat disconnected more slowly. I did not, she thought, intend to say that. And maybe I'm the one who needs to move on.

It only served to demonstrate how on edge she felt, and how insecure, and she wasn't used to that. Didn't know how to handle it.

Next I'll be snapping at the clients, she thought wryly as she closed down her computer. I need to be careful. And to keep my mind on my work. This is the life I've chosen, after all, so I should nurture it.

Dorita from Accounting appeared in her doorway. 'We're off to the wine bar. Coming with us?'

Cat pulled a face. 'I'm still a little whacked from the weekend.'

'Then what you need,' Dorita told her cheerfully, 'is some of the hair of the dog that took your leg off. Cindy and Megs are in a champagne mood.'

'And why shouldn't they be?' Cat slipped her arms into the jacket of her dark work suit. 'Sounds good to me. What are we celebrating?'

Dorita shrugged. 'The start of another working week. The fact that Megs has met a fella and thinks he's the one. Just pick a number.' She fluttered her fingers and vanished.

Cat didn't feel like a heavy after-work session, but the prospect of going home to an empty flat to brood had no great appeal either.

I need, she thought, a suitable distraction. And this could be it. Besides, as one of the firm's directors, it was a good thing for her to stay in touch with her junior colleagues. They were a talented and hard-working bunch, and immensely loyal in a marketplace where every contract had to be fought for.

With the shadow of recession never far away, people were reluctant to invest enormous sums in upgrading their working environments, and ImageMakers were maintaining their position by offering sensible, workable designs, using quality sub-contractors, and keeping each project strictly within budget.

Their reputation was high, but it was still a struggle, and it was impossible to relax, even for a moment—except, of course, when work was over for the day.

Or over for some, Cat amended ruefully, looking at the bulging briefcase that was accompanying her home.

The wine bar was already filling up when they arrived, but they managed to grab one of the last tables and Cat bought the first bottle of champagne. Penance, she thought as she handed over her credit card, for being ratty with her father.

At first most of the chatter was work-related, but as they began to unwind it started to get more personal.

During a sudden lull, Megs leaned forward. 'So, how was your cousin's wedding? You did go, I suppose? Any tasty men there?'

Cat drank some wine as she considered her response.

'Loads of them,' she drawled at last. 'All of them, alas, with equally tasty women.'

She hoped that would be an end to it, but soon found she was out of luck. Cindy was getting married the following year, and wanted exhaustive details about the hotel and what it had to offer. Megs, who seemed to be on the verge of having stars in her eyes, demanded a full description of Belinda's bridal gown. So she had little choice but to comply with their demands for information.

Maybe I can use it as a kind of exorcism, she thought wryly.

By the time she'd finished the bottle was empty, and Dorita was at the bar buying further supplies.

This would be the perfect opportunity to slip away, Cat thought, reaching for her bag, which hung from a hook under the table. As she straightened, she saw that Dorita was on her way back, and that her place at the counter had been taken by a tall man with dark, curling hair, wearing an elegant charcoal suit.

His back was turned to them all, but Cat felt herself freeze, her gaze fixed on him with painful incredulity.

Oh God, she thought. It can't be him—it can't...

'Did you spot him, girls? The new guy at the bar?' Dorita rolled her eyes. 'I've never seen him in here before, but seriously fanciable, I'd say.'

'And already fancied, by the look of it.' Cindy nodded significantly at the petite blonde who was threading her way towards him through the crowd.

Cat felt as if she'd been turned to stone as the girl joined him, sliding her arm through his with possessive familiarity. She wanted to look away. She longed to get up and run, but doubted whether she was capable of making it to the door. Her legs felt weak, and hurt seemed to be punching holes in her stomach.

Then he turned slightly, smiling as he bent to kiss his companion, and she realised that he was a complete stranger.

She swallowed, her body sagging in relief. What on earth had she been thinking of? she berated herself silently. This guy didn't bear even a passing resemblance to Liam. He was shorter, for one thing, and his shoulders weren't as broad. How could she not have realised?

If every glimpse of a tall, dark man is going to reduce me to bug-eyed paralysis, I'm in real trouble, she told herself impatiently. I need to get a grip. Claw my life back from this limbo.

'Are you all right, Cat?' Megs was studying her. 'You look as if you've seen a ghost.'

Cat forced a laugh. 'Nothing so romantic. I've just remembered I'm nearly out of milk and everything else, and I need to fit in a trip to the supermarket on my way home. So I'd better get going.'

She firmly refused any more champagne, and headed for the door. On the way, she stole a glance at the bar, wondering how she could have been such a fool. The pretty blonde was chatting animatedly to some people beside her, showing off the sparkling ring on her left hand, but he was leaning against the counter, looking round him.

As his glance met Cat's it sharpened with unconcealed interest, stripping her naked as it swept her from head to foot. He gave her an ingratiating grin, and lifted his glass in a furtive toast.

My God, Cat thought in revulsion. Someone attractive and apparently sane has staked her future on this piece of human debris.

And who was to say that Liam wasn't standing in another bar, looking into some other girl's eyes, telling her what a lousy weekend he'd had and how lonely he'd been without her?

The thought nearly made her gag. She half stumbled into the street, drawing deep breaths of stale air as she tried to recover her equilibrium.

She had to put the events of the weekend behind her, before

they drove her crazy, and she knew it. But if only someone would tell her how.

She couldn't face the struggle with the Underground, she thought, hailing a cab. She got out at her neighbourhood supermarket and wandered the aisles with her trolley, trying to summon up some interest in feeding herself over the coming week. In the end she settled for the usual staples, adding a cold roast chicken, pâté and salad, as well as dried pasta.

Spaghetti carbonara would be quick and easy tonight, she thought as she turned the corner towards her block of flats.

She was just fitting her key into the door when her neighbour emerged from the flat opposite, smiling over a dozen cellophane-wrapped red roses.

'For you, dear. You've got an admirer,' she added roguishly. *And not before time* was clearly the silent coda to that.

At any other time Cat would have found it amusing, but she was too stunned to do anything other than mutter a word of thanks through dry lips, and carry the flowers into the flat.

'Have dinner with me,' begged the message on the card in a florist's rounded script. 'Thursday 8 p.m. at Mignonette.'

There was no signature, but they had to be from Liam, she thought, her heart thudding wildly. Somehow, once his anger had cooled, he'd found out where she lived and was making contact—and far sooner than she could ever have dreamed. Her throat was constricted with excitement mixed with incredulity as she put her shopping in the kitchen and took a tall vase from a cupboard with hands that shook a little.

At the same time she had to suppress a tiny pang of disappointment that he'd fallen into the red rose cliché trap. And he was also assuming that she'd automatically be free on Thursday.

Which I am, she thought, but that's not the point.

Because he'd not offered her any way to communicate with him in turn, she realised. So she would have to choose whether to arrive meekly at the rendezvous—and she didn't do meek—or to stand him up, which she guessed would sever any connection between them for ever.

Well, I don't have to decide at once, she told herself as she arranged her flowers, and carried them back into the living room.

But in her heart she already knew what her decision would be, and she threw her head back and laughed with jubilant anticipation.

It seemed, of course, as if Thursday would never come. During the days, Cat was positive and dynamic, throwing herself into her work with renewed energy, her expectations carrying her along. But her nights were very different. She slept fitfully, her dreams wild and disturbing with an undercurrent of sensuality that often woke her, her body on fire, and a moan of sheer yearning on her lips.

'Mignonette, eh?' said Dorita, the company's restaurant guru, responding to Cat's studiedly casual query. She whistled. 'It must be a heavy date, Cat, because it's the top place for couples right now.' She observed Cat's flushed face with benevolent interest. 'Going there tonight?'

Cat shook her head. 'Tomorrow.'

Tonight, she thought ruefully, was her twosome with her mother at the Savoy—something she would have happily foregone.

But Vanessa greeted her with a radiant smile and champagne cocktails.

'Darling.' She kissed Cat on both cheeks, then stood back to scrutinise her plain grey shift dress with its matching jacket. She nodded. 'You look wonderful,' she approved.

'And so do you,' Cat returned with total sincerity, returning her embrace. Her mother seemed to have shed years since the weekend. The almost palpable tensions had disappeared, and she had that magical look of being lit with inner happiness that had been missing for so long.

If this was Gil's doing then Cat could only be grateful, in spite of her reservations about him.

Or did she simply recognise it because she shared it?

'I went down to see Susan yesterday,' Vanessa said when they were seated at their table, with their first course of seafood ravioli in front of them. 'She's planning to sell the house and move to France when everything's settled.'

Cat put down her fork, her eyes widening. 'She's really divorcing Uncle Robert? That's rather quick, isn't it?'

Vanessa shrugged. 'She says that when it's over, it's over, and she doesn't want to waste a moment of the rest of her life. She taught French before her marriage, and has always wanted a place there, only Robert wouldn't consider it.'

Cat shook her head. 'I had no idea.'

'Obviously there's more than one actress in the family,' Vanessa said drily, and applied herself to her food.

'But won't she be lonely?' Cat persisted.

'I wouldn't think so for a minute,' her mother said with a touch of asperity. 'She's still a very attractive woman. Once she's got Robert out of her system I can see her having a whale of a time.'

Cat raised her eyebrows. 'With you, no doubt, acting as her mentor?' she suggested.

Vanessa laughed. 'Not I, darling. At long last I'm planning to settle down for good, and I refuse to be distracted from that.' She gave Cat a long look. 'Well—I didn't expect you to turn cartwheels in the Savoy, but I thought you'd be a little pleased to hear I was aiming for respectability.'

With Gil, Cat thought, aghast. *With a muscle-bound toyboy? Oh, God, is this what she wants to tell me? Why she brought me here tonight for a girlie chat? And I was scared she just wanted to have another go about my father.*

She felt infinitely depressed, but managed to summon a smile. 'If that's really what you want,' she said quietly, 'I wish you every happiness.'

Vanessa stretched a manicured hand across the table and

laid it on Cat's. 'And I wish the same for you, dearest.' Her voice was oddly gentle. She paused. 'Just don't take as long as I've done to find it.'

Cat looked down at her plate. 'I'm perfectly content with my life, Ma.' *And in twenty-four hours' time I could be on the edge of bliss,* she added, silently and exultantly.

But less than twenty-four hours later much of her exhilaration had evaporated as she searched despairingly through her wardrobe, trying to find something which would look good without seeming as if she was trying too hard.

Eventually she decided on a cream georgette skirt, cut on the bias, with a matching jersey top, short-sleeved and round-necked, and a plain jacket the colour of sapphire. She put gold studs in her ears, and a tiny sapphire pendant in the shape of a star nestled at the base of her throat. She wore her favourite pale rose lipstick, and her nails were varnished in a similar shade.

She drew a deep breath as she looked at herself in the bedroom mirror.

'You'll do,' she said aloud.

It would have been far more cool to arrive late, she knew, but her taxi delivered her at Mignonette punctual to the second.

She paid off the driver and walked slowly into the restaurant.

She saw him at once, standing at the bar with a drink in his hand, and this time her eyes did not deceive her. He was wearing casual dark grey pants, and an open necked shirt that was almost silver. His jacket was slung across one shoulder. He was talking to the barman, and not looking at the door, so she could feast her eyes on him as greedily as she wished.

For a moment she indulged herself to the hilt, then started towards him, her stomach churning and a tight knot of excitement in her chest.

'Cat—you came.' A man's voice intruded into her happy

dream. Someone stood blocking her way. 'I was so afraid you'd turn me down.'

Dazed, Cat focused on him, her brows snapping together as recognition followed.

Oh, God, she thought. It's Tony, the best man.

'This is just so great.' He was smiling happily, oblivious to her sudden pallor as shock and disappointment kicked in. 'Have you been here before? One of the guys at work rec-ommended it. Our table's ready, so we may as well go in,' he added eagerly. 'We can have a drink while we're ordering. Better than standing at the bar.'

But then, anything was better than standing at this bar.

'Yes.' It didn't even sound like her voice. 'Yes, of course.'

As she followed him, putting one foot somehow in front of the other, like a mechanical doll, she risked one swift glance at Liam.

He had turned, probably to see what all the excitement was about, as Tony had not lowered his voice. The world shrank suddenly to enclose them in some echoing void, and their eyes met in one stunned, coruscating flash.

I thought it was you. She wanted to shout the words aloud in her despair. It should have been you.

But she said nothing, making herself look straight ahead, her silence drowning Tony's chatter.

Then they were moving under the archway into the restaurant, but Cat could still feel Liam's gaze burning into her back every step of the way, until, at last, she was safely out of his range of vision.

CHAPTER SIX

'DID you like the flowers?' asked Tony.

Cat, who'd been sitting gazing unseeingly at the menu, started. 'Thank you—they were amazing.' She thought of the long stiff stalks, and the still tightly furled, scentless crimson buds. 'But why didn't you sign the card?'

'Cheryl was always complaining I wasn't very romantic.' He spoke defensively. 'I thought I'd try a touch of mystery— and it worked.' He smiled at her, flushing slightly. 'Because here you are.'

'Indeed I am.' And wishing that she could be anywhere else in the world, she thought wretchedly.

Oh, God, she whispered inwardly. How can this be happening to me? How could I have jumped to the conclusion that the flowers had to be from Liam? And the message.

Well, wishful thinking was the short answer to that. She'd wanted it so badly to be him that she'd suspended rational thought. Ignored the bitter rancour of their parting. And poor Tony, of course, had simply passed through her consciousness without touching the edges. She hadn't given him a single thought, or anyone else either. Had never doubted her own conviction for a moment.

But she could have borne the disappointment somehow if only Liam had not been here—waiting, she'd thought, for her.

Oh, why—*why* should he choose to visit this particular restaurant out of all others on this particular night? Cat wailed silently. It was crazy—impossible. *Cruel.*

On the other hand, there wasn't the slightest reason for him not to patronise Mignonette. It was high-profile and popular. The date of his visit was just one of life's bitter ironies.

She supposed in a perverse way she should be thankful for

Tony's intervention. Otherwise she would have walked straight to Liam and probably suffered a crushing humiliation in the process.

And now she had to sit here, pretending to take an interest in food and wine when in truth she was wired up, every sense in overdrive, as she waited for Liam to enter the restaurant itself.

Mignonette was a series of rooms, opening out from each other, all decorated in cool pastels and divided into booths. The lights were shaded, the conversation hushed, and a pianist just inside the archway was softly playing a medley of romantic standards.

All in all, it was an ideal place for lovers, but not so good if you were here with entirely the wrong man.

And downright bad when you knew the man you really wanted was going to walk past your table at any moment.

It was like knowing a gun was about to go off, she told herself. You were excited and scared all at the same time. And hoping against hope that you wouldn't receive a fatal wound.

'I got your address from Freddie at the reception,' Tony went on, a faint note of self-congratulation in his tone. 'He was tickled pink at the thought of us getting together.'

But we're not together, she thought. And we never would be in a thousand years, even though you're good-looking, well-dressed, pleasant and a serious earner. And if Belinda doesn't murder bloody Freddie, I might have a go.

She sipped her dry martini. She said lightly, 'Then that makes everything all right.'

'Freddie and Belinda will be great,' he said after a pause. 'He can be a bit of a fool sometimes, but she'll make him toe the line.'

I bet she's already started, Cat thought drily, remembering her cousin's set face as she departed on honeymoon.

She heard approaching footsteps and tensed, knowing beyond all doubt who it was. She began to concentrate so furiously on the *à la carte* section that the words blurred and danced in front of her eyes.

He walked past without even a glance in her direction. He was not alone, and of course she had not expected him to be. But, all the same, she'd hoped so badly...

The girl with him was tall and slim, with long chestnut hair confined at the nape of her neck with a bow of black ribbon. Her skirt was black too, and the silk tunic she wore over it was striped in black and white. She had good legs, and moved well. And Cat didn't have to get a direct look at her face to know that she would be strikingly beautiful.

She would also have known her again anywhere, even if she was blind and in the dark. The image of them walking together into the adjoining room was etched with razor sharpness into her mind.

But at least they weren't sitting at the next table, and she had to be thankful for that, at least. Her voice was over-bright as she told Tony she would have the queen scallops, followed by *poulet Normande*.

Tony ordered *cassoulet*. 'Peasant food,' he said with satisfaction.

Very rich peasants, if they can afford these prices, thought Cat wearily, wondering how soon she could make an excuse and leave.

The food was delicious, but she ate embarrassingly little, simply pushing it round her plate. She barely touched the wine either, confining herself to sips of mineral water.

I should have done the same the other night, she thought wearily. Then I wouldn't be sitting here with a knife twisting inside me.

Although it was wrong to blame alcohol for her passionate surrender to Liam. It had been sheer, stark animal attraction that had brought them together. Fusing them into an explosion of physical desire which she'd never experienced before and had been unable to resist.

I made my choices, she thought flatly, and now I have to live with the consequences.

Tony, she noticed, had none of her reservations about the wine. He quickly finished off the first bottle and asked for a second.

The wine loosened his tongue, too. When they'd first sat down they'd talked about work, which Cat had found infinitely preferable to discussing more personal matters. But a chance remark of hers about lawyers had opened the floodgates, and she found herself being treated to a blow-by-blow account of divorce in the twenty-first century. He was clearly labouring under a strong sense of injury, and before too long Cat wanted to scream.

'Somebody's making Cheryl do this,' he kept declaring truculently. 'She doesn't need the money.'

By the time the second bottle was only a memory his speech was slurred, and he was beginning to get amorous, and a little maudlin.

Not an ideal combination, Cat thought, signalling discreetly to the waiter. But a perfect excuse to forego dessert.

She paid the bill, then, with the waiter's help, and praying that Liam would stay well out of the way and not witness her struggles, she managed to get Tony outside without causing too much fuss, and into a cruising cab. He tried tipsily to persuade her to accompany him, but she declined tersely, freeing herself forcefully from his wandering hand.

And a minute later another cab was speeding her in the opposite direction. Back to safety.

She leaned back in her corner and closed her eyes. 'Thank God that's over,' she muttered under her breath, somewhere between laughter and tears, then paused, the breath catching in her throat as she recognised the fuller implications of her words.

Her hands clenched together in her lap, and she turned to look out of the window in an attempt to refocus her thoughts on the brightly lit shops they were passing. But all in vain.

The only thing she was aware of was her own reflection in the glass—a pale girl, with quivering lips and an ocean's depth of pain in her eyes. And from that there was no distraction—and no retreat.

Cat walked into her flat the following evening, closed the door and leaned back against it, her shoulders slumped in weariness. The weekend stretched ahead of her like a desert, punctuated only by such excitements as dusting, vacuuming, and doing some laundry.

She might even stir up a frenzy by sorting her DVDs into alphabetical order. Hell. She pulled a face. How sad was that?

One thing she was determined on. She was not going to cry herself to sleep for a second time tonight. As soon as she'd turned off her lamp the previous evening all the suppressed emotion had come welling up inside her and she'd started to sob hopelessly—desperately—her tears soaking the pillow.

And even when exhaustion had finally claimed her there had been no respite. She'd woken near dawn to find her face wet again, and the taste of salt on her lips.

So, she would start as she meant to go on tonight—plan her evening like a campaign. A relaxing bath, she thought, with the new toiletries that held no inconvenient memories, then into the dear old velour robe. Some music, naturally—probably Mozart. And, because she'd had lunch with a potential client, just a light supper. A cheese omelette, maybe, with a glass of wine. And then she'd get her laptop and start mapping out some preliminary ideas for the new suite of offices, which had been the reason for the lunch. That should fill the time nicely.

Even two weeks ago I'd have been perfectly content with an evening like that, she told herself. And I can be again. I just need to take control.

She put on the horn concerto while her bath was running, then lay back in the water, hair pinned on top of her head, eyes closed, letting the glorious notes drive any lingering demons from her soul.

She was safely covered in her comfort blanket, and on her way to the kitchen, when her doorbell sounded. She paused, frowning slightly, wondering who the caller could be. God forbid it should be Tony, come to do penance.

She was in two minds whether to answer the door or not when she remembered that it might be her neighbour, with a parcel that she'd taken in. Those books, perhaps, that Cat had ordered on the Internet.

As the bell sounded again she called, 'Yes, I'm here.' She dealt swiftly with the safety lock and flung open the door.

'I'm sorry,' she began, then stopped dead, her eyes dilating in shock and the apologetic smile fading as she saw who was confronting her.

'Good evening,' Liam said quietly. He was in full City gear this evening—dark blue suit with a faint pinstripe, crisp white shirt and silk tie. His face was unsmiling and weary, his mouth taut.

Her voice was small and hoarse. 'What—what are you doing here?'

'I hardly know myself.' There was a dull flare of colour along the high cheekbones. 'I swore that I wouldn't do this, but it seems I no longer have a choice.'

He flung back his head and looked at her, the smoky eyes cool and unflinching. He said, 'If the offer you made me is still open, then I'll take it. I want you, and I'll pay any price to have you.'

She shook her head. 'I—I don't understand.'

'You suggested we should meet,' Liam said evenly. 'On neutral territory and in comparative anonymity in order to pursue our mutual enjoyment of each other. At the time, I didn't agree.'

His mouth hardened. 'Since then I've had plenty of opportunity to think,' he continued. 'And I accept your terms. All of them.'

He paused. 'But it's up to you to say whether you still want this or not. And naturally I'll abide by your decision. If you send me away, you won't hear from me again.'

There was a silence. Her mind was whirling as she tried to take in what he'd said. To understand it.

He'd offered her a get-out clause, she realised numbly. She could tell him she'd made a mistake—even that it had all been a joke which had misfired—and he would be out of her life for ever, and she could return to some approximation of peace and normality. Perhaps.

Instead, she heard herself say shakily, 'What's made you decide to—throw down the gauntlet like this?'

'Seeing you again last night,' Liam said levelly. 'Knowing that all my efforts to put you out of my head had been completely useless. Although, my God, I tried,' he added with feeling.

Her voice sank to a whisper. 'So did I.'

There was another silence. He said carefully, 'Do I take it, then, that the answer's yes?'

She nodded, swiftly and jerkily, not looking at him. She said, 'Do you—would you—like to come in?'

'No,' he said, his mouth twisting. 'No, I don't think so. It's probably best if we obey your rules from the outset. And you want our encounters to be on neutral territory.'

'We also said no personal details.' She swallowed. 'Yet you've clearly discovered where I live.'

'Yes,' he said. 'But that was before I knew there were any rules, and even longer before I agreed to obey them.'

'So how did you get my address? From the hotel?'

'Yes.'

Cat bit her lip, remembering the pretty receptionist who'd manned the desk on Saturday evening. 'Using your famous powers of persuasion, no doubt?'

He shrugged equably. 'If you say so. But from now on I won't cheat. We'll keep our meetings strictly elsewhere.'

She went on staring at him. She said slowly, 'My hotel bill. Was there really a problem with the computer?'

Liam propped a shoulder against the doorframe, a faint ruefulness in his expression. 'Who knows? There often is. That's what computers are like.'

'You—really went to all those lengths?' Cat shook her head. 'I can't believe it.'

'Believe it and more.' His voice was almost fierce. 'I needed to see you again. I didn't want you to turn into the Cat that walked by herself and slip away until I'd had a chance to talk you round to my point of view.' He paused. 'Am I eternally condemned for that?'

'No,' she said. 'I think it's a little late for that.'

Liam nodded. 'So, do you trust me to find somewhere sufficiently neutral for our first rendezvous?'

Just like that? Cat thought bewilderedly. Without even a kiss or a touch? As if he was arranging a business appointment?

'Yes,' she said, numbly. 'That would be—fine.'

He took a personal organiser from his inside pocket and scanned through it. 'Next Thursday would be good for me.' He glanced up. 'How about you?'

'Yes.' She still had that curious sense of disbelief—of detachment. 'Yes, I can manage that.'

'Then that's agreed.' His smile was brief and formal. 'I'll send a car for you at ten o'clock. Until then.'

Send a car—as if she was a parcel to be collected? And at ten? Clearly there was to be no leisurely wooing over dinner this time.

He was actually turning away when she said his name.

'Did I forget something?' His brows lifted in enquiry.

So many things, Cat thought, swallowing. *But there's a barrier, suddenly, and I can't get round it. I can't reach you.*

She clutched at a straw. Forced a smile of her own. 'I wanted to mention last night—to explain...'

'But you don't have to do that,' he said, quite gently, but

with a faint trace of something like mockery in his voice. 'Under the rules we see each other when we wish, but the rest of our lives remain a closed book. And the beauty of that is no excuses or explanations. We can both do exactly as we like.'

So he doesn't care about Tony, she thought, with a touch of bleakness. But I'm not allowed to ask about his companion either, and that's a different story.

'Yes,' she said, her voice faintly constricted. 'Yes, of course.'

He lingered, his meditative gaze considering her in silence, and she suddenly realised what he was seeing—her face scrubbed as clean as a child's, without a trace of cosmetic, and surrounded by the damp tendrils which had escaped from her pinned-up hair. The elderly velour dressing gown, kind as an old friend, but undoubtedly sacrificing beauty to comfort, however you looked at it. Not a speck of allure anywhere.

Her hand went almost protectively to the base of her throat, drawing the worn edges of the robe together.

She looked back at him, her chin lifting in challenge. 'Having second thoughts?'

'Having all kinds of thoughts,' Liam returned coolly. 'Which I look forward to sharing with you on Thursday night. I can hardly wait. And wear something glamorous,' he added softly. 'Something I'll enjoy removing.' His smile touched her like an intimate caress. 'Goodnight.'

Ridiculously, she found herself blushing. Felt a warm tide of colour spread up from her toes to her forehead, and knew it would not have escaped his attention, or his amusement.

Wordlessly, she stepped backwards and closed the door between them. She sagged against the frame, her breathing ragged, her heartbeat tumultuous.

My God, she thought, swallowing. This was pragmatism carried to the nth degree.

She made herself walk over to the sofa and sat down in its corner, her feet curled under her.

What am I getting into here? she wondered incredulously. Some kind of business arrangement controlled by dates and logistics—efficient but passionless?

No, she thought, remembering his smile, and the sudden, sensuous glint in his eyes that had so rocked her. Certainly not passionless. But maybe not very romantic either.

If she was honest, she realised, she'd never considered the practical details of her idea until this very moment. But Liam had brought them home to her, loud and clear. She felt suddenly cold, and pulled the folds of the robe around her.

But she wished he'd accepted her tacit invitation to stay the night, and that he was here at this moment, beside her, his lips weaving warm magic on her skin. His body pressing hers deeper and deeper into the yielding cushions. His flesh against hers. Within hers.

She was aware of the deep burn of desire igniting inside her. She lifted her clenched fist to her mouth and bit the knuckle with almost clinical precision.

Fighting one pain with another, she told herself in self-derision.

I should have tempted him to stay—used my own powers of persuasion, she thought.

But maybe that was outside the bounds of possibility, Cat told herself, stifling a sigh. Perhaps Liam wasn't turned on by the plain, unvarnished version of her he'd seen tonight. Instead, he wanted his mistress-to-be smoothed out, made-up, and perfectly presented. Scented and beddable.

Well, she thought, she'd wanted a secret no-strings liaison, and this was precisely what she was getting, so she could hardly complain.

This time the sigh escaped her, telling in its wistfulness. And its longing.

One thing was certain, she thought, rallying herself, she'd completely lost her appetite for supper. So she might as well go to bed, even if it was alone, and try to get some rest.

Although instinct warned her that sleep might be elusive

and her dreams thoroughly disturbing, keeping her tossing and turning until dawn. And instinct, as it turned out, was absolutely right.

Work proved to be Cat's salvation in the days that followed. She tried to fill every hour with at least seventy minutes, scheduling site visits, meeting potential sub-contractors, and following up on even the most unpromising enquiries. And she'd never been so up to date on her paperwork either.

She tried hard to put the coming Thursday night out of her mind, but not with any real success. Liam was never far away, waiting on the edge of her consciousness, making her body sing with tension.

It was ridiculous to feel so nervous, she castigated. He was the lover she'd dreamed of, and he was going to be hers—on her terms. What more could she ask?

Well, she might have wished the arrangement hadn't been quite so businesslike, but again she was hardly entitled to complain.

She wasn't working on Thursday itself. She was owed several days' extra vacation, and she planned to use one of them pampering herself at a health spa with every beauty treatment known to the mind of woman.

And in accordance with his request—or was it a demand?—she'd bought herself something glamorous: a housecoat in heavy black silk, long-sleeved, floor-length and full-skirted, fastened by a long row of tiny buttons that began at the deep V of the neckline and ended at mid-thigh.

She was folding it in tissue and placing it in her overnight bag on Wednesday evening when the doorbell rang.

Cat froze, sending herself a horrified glance in the mirror. Oh, no, she besought any passing fate, he can't have caught me again, with wet hair and wearing the comfort blanket.

She opened the door carefully, using the chain, and peeped round the edge. A young man was standing there in leathers, carrying a crash helmet under his arm and holding a padded envelope.

'Miss Adamson? I've been asked to deliver this, and wait for an answer if needed.'

He passed the yellow envelope through the gap to Cat, who tore it open. Three keys on a ring with a metal tag slid into the palm of her hand. The attached label read 'Flat 2, 53 Wynsbroke Gardens'. And, scrawled underneath the address in Liam's distinctive writing, 'In case I'm late.' She stared down at it. So, she thought, this was to be the meeting place he'd arranged—not the anonymous hotel room she'd expected, but a flat in one of London's most expensive areas. Serious stuff.

She swallowed convulsively. My God, she told herself. It's coming true. It's really happening. I don't think I believed it until this moment.

Yet here was the incontrovertible truth. Liam had meant everything he said. Her hand closed round the keys so tightly that the metal dug into her hand as she stared unseeingly in front of her.

I'm scared, she realised in bewilderment. I'm actually *scared*. And how pathetic is that?

'Is there an answer, miss?' The messenger's voice reached her from the passage outside.

I'm being offered another choice, she thought. Another chance to do the wise thing. All I have to do is hand back the keys, say there's been some mistake, and I'm out of it for good. He won't try again. And I'll be safe. Safe...

The word echoed longingly in her head.

She took a deep breath. 'Thank you,' she said quietly. 'But there's no reply.'

My decision, she thought as she closed the door, is made.

'You're very tense,' the masseuse said disapprovingly, her hands working essential oils into Cat's neck and shoulders.

'I have a lot on my mind,' Cat returned wryly.

She'd had a wonderful facial, she'd been manicured, ped-
icured, and taken a sauna. By this time she should have been
totally relaxed and floating, her mind free, looking forward to
a night of pleasure. Instead she was as taut as a guitar string,
and almost ready to snap.

I'm heading for disaster, she thought, biting her lip.

In many ways it might have been more sensible to have
spent a normal day at work. At least she would have been
forced to concentrate her mind on something apart from the
evening ahead.

Yet here she was, being waxed, plucked, smoothed and
scented as if her life depended on it.

I feel, she thought moodily, like some harem girl who's
been summoned by the Sultan. And I wonder what the Sultan
would have said if the harem had started summoning him
instead. Probably had the lot of them tied up in sacks and
chucked into the Bosphorus. Where, of course, they would
have sunk without trace.

And that's what I'm risking too. That sooner or later, when
all passion's spent, I'll be left alone and floundering. And how
will I bear it?

But I mustn't think like that. It's the beginning of the affair,
not the end. I'm getting what I want, and I should be happy
about it.

'You're clearly under a lot of stress,' the masseuse told her
as they parted. 'Maybe you should consider having regular
treatments.'

I hope I won't need them, Cat returned silently, murmuring
something non-committal. As she was putting her credit card
away, after paying the bill, she heard the clink of the keys in
the bottom of her bag. Flat 2, 53 Wynsbroke Gardens, she
repeated silently, as she'd been doing all day. As if there was
any real chance of her forgetting.

She'd planned to go straight home, of course. Told herself
that bringing the keys with her had been some kind of mild
aberration and was of no importance. But that didn't explain

why she found herself turning right instead of left at the traffic lights, and heading straight for Notting Hill.

She found Wynsbroke Gardens without difficulty, and managed to squeeze into a parking space some two hundred yards away round the nearest corner.

She walked back slowly, counting the numbers on the houses until she reached number 53. She simply wanted to look at it, that was all, she told herself in self-justification. Just to see where Liam had chosen for this strange tryst. She hadn't the slightest intention of going in, of course.

Number 53 turned out to be a tall house, part of a terrace, with a flight of stone steps leading up to a pillared portico, and narrower stairs going down to a basement.

There was an entry system by the front door, but there was no name beside the buzzer for Flat 2.

I'll try one key, Cat thought. And if it doesn't fit I'll walk away. Wait until tonight.

But the key did fit, and she stepped forward into a tiled hallway. The entrance to the ground floor flat was on her left, and there was another door straight ahead bearing a brass number two on its gleaming surface.

Once inside, a flight of carpeted stairs led up to yet another door.

I'm beginning to feel like Bluebeard's wife, Cat mocked herself, fitting the third key into the lock. Beyond lay a passage with pastel walls and seagrass flooring.

Cat hesitated momentarily, then turned right, opening the door at the end. She found herself in a large sunlit room, with long windows and a balcony overlooking the communal gardens below.

The floorboards had been stripped and waxed, and the walls were painted a pale cream. Two deeply cushioned sofas upholstered in dark green flanked a marble fireplace, and a dining area with a table, four chairs and a small sideboard had been created in an alcove at the far end of the room.

The whole place had that pristine just-decorated look. It

was also curiously vacant. Apart from a tray of bottles with some crystal tumblers on the sideboard, there was nothing there. Not a picture on any of the walls, or an ornament on one of the surfaces. Not even a clock on the mantelpiece. Even the furniture looked brand-new, as if no one had ever sat on one of those cushions or eaten a meal at the polished table.

It was undeniably a beautiful room, Cat thought, yet the effect was almost soulless.

The main bedroom opened out of the living room. The wide bed had already been made up, Cat realised, her heart missing a beat, and the tailored blue coverlet was turned back to reveal crisp white linen.

Well, at least the priorities had been dealt with, she thought, her mouth twisting as she noted that soap and towels had been laid out in the gleaming bathroom next door.

Cat found herself backing out again, almost on tiptoe, as if she'd entered a church in the middle of some service. Absurd, she told herself as she crossed the living room again, deliberately letting her shoes clatter noisily on the wooden floor.

She found the kitchen at the other end of the passage. It had a full range of fitted units and appliances above and below the granite work surface, but all the drawers and cupboards were unused, and the refrigerator was empty.

It's just a very elegant shell, Cat thought bleakly, with no clue about who it might belong to. In fact, it doesn't look as if anyone's ever lived here at all, least of all Liam.

Perhaps he had flats like this across London, she thought, biting her lip. Blank, transitory boxes where he entertained his women.

No, she told herself abruptly. That's nonsense. After all, this was all my idea, not his. And I was the one who specified it had to be neutral territory too.

Well, he's done me proud. This is about as utilitarian and *neutral* as it's possible to get.

What did I expect, anyway? A heart-shaped bed with black

silk sheets and mirrors on the ceiling? A fur rug in front of a
blazing fire?

She sighed. So, it was hardly a love nest, but at least she
could make it rather less of an echoing void.

She took the car up to Notting Hill Gate. In the supermarket
she bought staples, like bread, milk and eggs, then added ba-
con, smoked salmon, fresh raspberries, cream, coffee and a
couple of bottles of champagne. She also bought an armful
of lilies and carnations, and a tall dark green vase to put them
in.

Back at the flat, she stocked the fridge neatly, then arranged
her flowers, which she set in the centre of the dining table.
By the time she left their scent was already beginning to per-
meate through the warm air, making the place a little less
bleak.

But it's still nothing like home, she thought as she got back
in the car—and stopped herself right there with a gasp.
Because that was the whole point—wasn't it?

And now she simply had to make the best of it, she told
herself. And shivered.

CHAPTER SEVEN

THE car Liam sent for her was long, dark and powerful, and punctual to the second. Which was just as well, Cat thought as she handed her overnight case to the driver, because her nerves by this time were stretched to screaming point.

Her chauffeur was a polite, taciturn man, in a neat grey suit with a peaked cap. Cat longed to ask him if he regularly delivered Liam's women to him, but didn't dare. In any case, the glass partition between him and the back of the car, where she sat almost on the edge of her seat, remained firmly closed.

What I really want is someone to take my hand and tell me everything's going to be all right, she thought, a bubble of near-hysteria rising in her throat. And I've never been that naïve. I'm still the Cat that Walks by Herself. I have to be.

She hadn't realised how much she was hoping that Liam would be there ahead of her, waiting to take her in his arms, until she unlocked the doors and found the flat still empty.

She drew the heavy cream curtains across the windows, and after a brief hesitation lit the gas fire in the marble hearth, telling herself it felt chilly now that darkness was here. Or was she just nervous?

Stagefright, she thought with a grimace, sitting back on her haunches and watching the flames flicker blue.

She took her case into the bedroom and extracted the new housecoat. It moulded her slenderness like a second skin, the skirts flaring into soft folds at her hips and falling open, mid-thigh, to reveal her slim legs. The unrelieved black emphasised the creaminess of her skin against the dipping neckline.

She studied her reflection in the long mirror, trying to see herself with his eyes.

It was undoubtedly seductive, she acknowledged restively,

but was it rather too obvious—especially against this minimalist background? Well, only time would tell.

And it was time that Liam was here. She needed his reassurance—the flare of passion in his eyes—the hunger of his mouth.

There was no television, no stereo or radio in the living room. Nothing, not even a magazine, to alleviate the tension of this endless waiting.

She was beginning to wonder if he'd changed his mind—or even if he'd planned all this as a cruel joke to punish her for daring to damage his male pride—when she heard the outer door open and slam shut, and his footsteps on the stairs.

She'd intended to be stretched on the sofa, cool and casual, her smile offering a welcome that was his alone. Instead, she found herself jumping to her feet, her clenched fists buried in the folds of her gown to conceal the fact that they were trembling.

He came slowly into the room, moving almost wearily, the smoky eyes guarded as they surveyed her.

'Good evening.' His voice was quiet, courteous, but it did not sing with desire, and he didn't come across to her as she'd hoped. 'I apologise for my lateness.'

She swallowed. 'It—it doesn't matter. You're here now,' she returned uncertainly. She paused. 'You look tired.'

'I am,' he said pleasantly. 'But not too exhausted to pay you the attention you deserve in bed, if that's what concerns you.'

'It isn't,' she denied swiftly. 'I simply thought you might like some coffee—or something to eat. I—I brought food.' She tried a smile. 'I make good scrambled eggs.'

'I don't doubt it,' Liam drawled, his expression suddenly cynical. 'But I didn't come here for your domestic abilities, my sweet, in case you've forgotten. I'm not hungry.' He shrugged off his suit jacket and tossed it over the arm of the sofa. 'Frankly, I've had a bitch of a day, but a hot bath should improve my mood considerably.'

He walked towards the bedroom, loosening his tie as he went, then paused. 'But you could bring me a drink,' he added softly. 'If you wanted. Shall we say in ten minutes?'

She nodded jerkily. 'Of course. Straight whisky?'

His brows lifted in faint mockery. 'You have a good memory.'

'But then,' she said, 'I've had little to do but remember.'

'And nor have I,' he said, his gaze reassessing her. Lingering without softening. 'And I haven't forgotten a thing.' His smile was tight. 'So—ten minutes, then.'

She'd noticed a good single malt among the bottles on the sideboard. She poured a generous shot into one of the tumblers, and sat down to wait.

Thumb-twiddling, she thought, her mouth twisting, had never been her favourite form of exercise, although she supposed she could always make herself useful and put his jacket on a hanger.

My God, she told herself in self-derision. He's been here five minutes, and I'm turning into his girlfriend.

She looked at the jacket again, more thoughtfully, then glanced towards the half-open door of the bedroom. There was no sign of movement, and the water running into the tub had stopped a few moments ago. By this time he would be in the bath.

And he knew so much about her, while her information about him was practically nil. She realised, of course, that he must be wealthy, but, oddly, that was the fact that interested her least.

There had to be clues in his pockets—his driving licence—his wallet. It wasn't a very honest and upright thing to do, perhaps, but, after all, he'd wheedled her name and address out of the hotel. Quid pro quo, she told herself.

There was no driving licence, but his wallet was in his inside pocket. She withdrew it deftly and began to look through it, searching for credit cards, business cards—anything that would tell her about him.

Just his name, she placated the god of sneaks. And maybe what he does for a living. That's all I want to know.

But she was to be disappointed. His wallet contained about a hundred pounds in cash, but no cards of any kind. Nothing that contained even a hint about his identity. Except, she realised, something that had become wedged in one of the small inner pockets. She retrieved it after a brief struggle, and saw it was a photograph, upside down.

His wife? she thought, staring down at it, reluctant to turn it over. His fiancée? His girlfriend? Whoever it was, he kept it well-hidden.

She would soon be running out of time, she thought, forcing herself to examine it. And if it was a woman she would only have herself to blame.

But it was a dog—a springer spaniel with an infectious grin—which looked back at her, and Cat cursed under her breath as she forced the snapshot back into its place and returned the wallet to his jacket.

Well, that was a total waste of time, she thought as she carried his Scotch into the bathroom, her skirts rustling around her.

Liam was lying back in the bath. His eyes were closed, but the almost haggard look she'd noticed earlier was beginning to fade.

She stood watching him for a moment, feeling her heart twist within her, then said quietly, 'I've brought your drink.'

He stirred, stretching a little, then sat up. 'Thank you.' He took the tumbler from her hand and placed it on the small table beside the bath. He surveyed her meditatively. 'Would you care to join me?'

She said, 'Thank you, but I don't drink whisky.'

'And that,' he said gently, 'is not what I meant—as I'm sure you know,' he added, his eyes glinting with amusement.

'Well.' A smile trembled on her lips in reply. 'Perhaps so.' And her hands went to the first tiny button on her bodice.

'No.' His voice was soft, but incisive. 'Leave it on. I wan
you just as you are. Or have you forgotten?'

She halted, staring at him, then down at herself. 'No, bu
my housecoat—it will be ruined.'

He leaned back, picking up the tumbler beside him and
swallowing some of its contents. 'But in a very good cause
Besides, it would never have had the same effect a second
time,' he added, his smile widening into a grin.

'Well…' Cat pretended to consider. 'Probably not.' She
climbed sedately into the bath and settled herself at the op
posite end, arranging her sodden skirts around her and trying
not to laugh. 'Your mood certainly has improved.'

'And that's not the only area of improvement, I promise.
he said, his eyes dancing wickedly. He put down his glass
and leaned forward, drawing her closer to him. He kissed her
his mouth moving on hers gently and sensuously, and her lip
parted on a sigh to allow him deeper access. When he lifted
his head at last they were both breathless, both trembling.

With infinite tenderness Liam's hand smoothed the silk
strands of hair back from her face, then travelled slowly dow
the line of her throat, and lower to the waiting row of button:
He began to release them one by one, slowly and gently, hi
gaze intent.

Cat was very still, her breathing still ragged, her cloude
eyes widening as he slowly uncovered her. Her nipples wen
hardening uncontrollably against the soft brush of the silk, th
sweet hidden depths of her womanhood aching for his pos
session.

As the last button gave way Liam pushed aside the loos
ened edges of the robe with a sharp indrawn breath, his eye
feasting on her with a hunger he did not bother to hide.

'You are loveliness itself.' His voice was husky, and a litt
strained.

She smiled at him as she shrugged the robe from her shou
ders, freed her arms from the damp cling of the sleeves an
let the ruined silk slide down into the water.

She moved closer to him, lifting herself on to her knees and straddling his thighs, her hands gripping his shoulders. She leaned forward, letting her mouth brush his, swiftly, teasingly.

With one hand she stroked the side of his throat, feeling the race of the strong pulse at its base.

Then, with her free hand, she began to touch herself lightly and pleasurably, in deliberate incitement, letting her fingers brush the dark rose peaks of her breasts then slide down to her belly, and the soft curls at the parting of her thighs. Hearing him groan softly in response as he watched her almost mesmerised.

She cupped his face in her hands and kissed him again, running her tongue softly along the inner fullness of his lower lip. Then she bent her head, licking his hot, flat nipples with the point of her tongue, while her hands strayed downwards, exploring the strength of his arousal with delicate greed.

Liam's arm circled her, supporting her spine like an iron bar as she leaned backwards, her eyes half closed, her fingers holding him, guiding him to her secret threshold. And as he entered her her body opened for him like a flower.

It was no leisurely possession. Their mutual need was too forceful—too driven for that. Her body echoed his thrusts almost frantically. She could already feel the spiral inside her uncoiling, carrying her upwards to rapturous oblivion.

'Is it safe?' The urgent words rasped from his throat.

Panting, wordless, she nodded, her hands gripping his shoulders, the only reality in a disintegrating world.

His hand slid down between them, seeking and finding her tiny hidden bud, coaxing it to an almost painful tumescence with the tips of his fingers. Taking her to the edge, and then, suddenly, beyond it.

She heard herself cry out in a cracked voice, her body shuddering violently as the spasms of pleasure engulfed her, and heard him answer, the sound torn from him. *'Catherine.'*

She felt herself collapse against him, lay wrapped in his arms, the surge of her heartbeat mingling with his.

'This water's getting cold,' Liam murmured into her ear eventually. 'Why don't we go to bed?'

She smiled against his skin. 'Why don't we, indeed? Oh, God,' she added as they slowly disentangled themselves. 'Have you seen the state of the floor?'

'Yes.' He was laughing as he helped her out of the bath. 'Careful you don't slip.' He took one of the towels from the rail and began to dry her, patting her skin gently.

She selected a towel of her own to use on him, learning him with her hands and loving it. 'Shouldn't we do something about it?'

'We can put these down when we've finished with them to soak up the worst.' He shrugged. 'But clearing up is someone else's job.'

'Oh.' She digested that, frowning. 'Liam, is this your flat?'

'No.' He smiled down at her. 'It's *our* flat.'

She said slowly, 'You mean you've—rented it? For us?'

'Yes,' he said, and paused. 'For as long as we want it.'

Cat's hands faltered a little. She was being reminded, she realised, that this was a strictly finite relationship.

She said hurriedly, 'But that's not really fair. You must let me make a contribution.'

He framed her face in his hands, kissing her mouth. 'You have,' he told her quietly. 'You're here.' He kissed her again. 'Now, come to bed with me and convince me all over again that I'm not dreaming.'

He took the towel from her unresisting hand and dropped it on to the wet floor to join his own, then lifted her into his arms and carried her into the lamplit room beyond.

She lay in his arms, her sweat-dampened body joined passionately to his, blind, mindless, oblivious to everything but the mounting crescendo of exquisite sensation that he was creating within her, her lips parting in a silent scream as her entire being splintered once more into ecstasy.

When she could speak, she said hoarsely, breathlessly, 'I—I never believed I could feel like this.'

'Or so often,' Liam murmured, his lips against her hair.

She twisted to look up at him suspiciously. 'You're laughing at me.'

'No, darling.' His hand stroked her shoulder, soothing her. 'Never at you. But with you, maybe.'

He drew her closer, fitting her against him as if it was what she'd been created for.

She relaxed into his embrace, her eyelids drooping. Making love with him was like being cast adrift on a river, she thought drowsily. Finding herself caught irresistibly in some strong but peaceful current, but only at first. Because the rapids were waiting, and beyond them the edge of the waterfall, lifting and tossing her out into its brilliance and thunder. And, at its foot, a deep, serene pool into which she was happy to sink, knowing that sunlight waited above the misty green water.

There would be kisses, she thought, as she surrendered to the dreamy aftermath of delight, and the skilful, beguiling caress of his hands leading her once more to pleasure. When she awoke in his arms.

But when she finally stirred it was to a very different reality. Because the bed beside her was empty, with the covers thrown back, and the room was no longer in darkness, as it had been when she fell asleep.

Suddenly she was aware of movement, and sat up, pushing her hair out of her eyes.

Liam was standing on the other side of the room, almost fully dressed and fitting links into the cuffs of his shirt.

Her voice was husky with bewilderment. 'What's happening? Where are you going?'

He looked at her, his brows drawing together in a frown of compunction. 'I didn't mean to disturb you, Cat. I'm sorry.'

'Sorry?' She shook her head, trying to clear it, and squinted at her watch. 'My God, it's half past two in the morning.' She stared at him. 'You're leaving? Already?'

'I must.' He began to knot his tie, swiftly and expertly. 'I have an early flight from Heathrow. Try and go back to sleep.'

She sat up, the covers sliding down from her body, and heard his short intake of breath as he looked at her uncovered breasts. Heard it, and smiled inwardly. Maybe he would be checking in late today—if he made the flight at all.

She lay back against the pillows, watching him through half-closed eyes. She said softly, 'I thought you'd be staying all night. That we'd have breakfast together. I'm—a little surprised.'

He gave her a level look. 'You wanted us to meet secretly to make love. And that's what we've done. I don't think breakfast was included in the terms.' He walked into the living room and came back with his jacket. 'Unless, of course, you want to renegotiate?' he added silkily.

'No,' she said lightly, concealing her sense of crushing disappointment. 'No, it's fine. After all, we both have busy lives.' She paused in her turn. 'I'm well satisfied with the arrangement,' she added demurely, her lashes veiling her eyes and a little smile playing round her mouth. Deliberately changing herself into the cat that got the cream, and making him know it. 'So far.'

His own smile was cool, and he did not come over to the bed to her, as she'd wanted, even expected. 'Happy to be of service, ma'am.'

'Except that it's still one-sided,' Cat went on, stretching luxuriously and allowing the sheet to slip even further. He might be leaving, she thought, but that was no reason to make it easy for him. 'You've found out my name, and where I live, whereas I don't know half as much about you.'

Liam pulled on his jacket, his mouth twisting in open amusement. 'I'd say we'd become very intimately acquainted,' he drawled. 'In fact, I might even let you call me Lee.'

'Thank you.' Cat bit her lip. 'But that's not what I meant.'

'But it's all that's on offer.' He allowed her a second to digest that, then took a card from his trouser pocket. 'I've ordered the car to pick you up at seven-thirty, but if you want to change that just ring this number.'

'There's no phone in the flat,' she said. 'I noticed.'

'However, I'm sure you never leave home without your mobile,' Liam said softly. 'And the car's booked in your name, so there's no point in questioning the driver,' he added, reading her mind with unforgivable accuracy.

And even less point in grinding her teeth, Cat told herself. Or picking up the bedside lamp and slinging it at him.

She said, 'You're very efficient.'

He shrugged. 'And you're the one who wants to keep things anonymous and exciting.' He smiled at her, his eyes travelling down her naked body with undisguised regret. 'And it's not working, my sweet. I still intend to catch my plane, so don't catch cold on my account.'

Cat gave him a mutinous glare and dragged the sheet up to her chin.

She said tautly, 'So, when shall we see each other again? Or am I not supposed to know that either?'

'I'll be in touch,' he said. He walked to the bed, bent and kissed her hard on the mouth. 'But from a safe distance, naturally.'

As he straightened Cat saw that he had produced his wallet, and was casually dangling it right in front of her. She found herself stiffening.

He looked down at her, his eyes glinting. 'And you have learned something about me tonight,' he told her. He tossed the wallet in the air and caught it, before replacing it in his pocket. 'Because you now know that I'm a dog lover,' he added gently. 'Don't you?'

Grinning, he blew her a kiss and went, leaving Cat staring after him, flushed, furious, and completely at a loss.

*   *   *

He had told her to go back to sleep, but that was easier said than done. Even with the lamp off, and the pillow punched viciously into shape, Cat found herself wide awake, her eyes burning into the darkness.

Liam was ahead of her at every turn, she thought bitterly. He'd known perfectly well she would seize the chance to look in his wallet, and had prepared the ground accordingly.

Because he was totally determined to keep her at arm's length, mentally and emotionally.

Well, she told herself, I asked for that. In fact, I demanded it, so I have only myself to blame. But that, somehow, makes it no easier to handle.

Because she now had to face the fact that her cunning plan was fundamentally flawed, and that she was the only one in the dark.

What made the situation even harder to bear was the realisation that she didn't just want to discover his name and address and what he did for a living. That was only the start.

I need to know everything about him, she thought, from the day he was born to the immediate present. I want to know where he is now, where he's planning to go, and what he's thinking. Above all, what he's thinking...

And if any painful secrets were uncovered along the way she would simply have to endure them, she thought with a sigh. But for now she had to cope with bewilderment and a deep and abiding loneliness.

She turned over, burying her face determinedly in the pillow. Sometimes she managed to doze a little, but inevitably woke again too soon, reaching across the width of the bed to find him, with tears scalding in her throat.

It had simply never occurred to her that they would not spend the entire night together. She'd believed that dawn would find them still in each other's arms. Imagined herself in the bath while he shaved, talking together. Even making plans, as lovers do. Until he had tacitly reminded her that this was no conventional love affair.

She'd even brought a frying pan and a coffee pot with her, and had planned to make scrambled eggs with smoked salmon for their breakfast. A mistake, she thought, with a pang, that she would not make again.

At last she gave up her attempts to sleep as a bad job, and decided to make her own preparations for leaving.

She finished mopping the bathroom floor with the discarded towels, then put them in the linen basket. She knelt beside the bath and began to wring out the saturated black silk. It was completely spoiled, but she would wrap it in one of the supermarket carriers and dispose of it at home, together with the unwanted food.

She would leave no trace of herself. No memory of last night. No anticipation of the future. From now on she would stick to the rules of their bargain and live only for the present.

Yet, in spite of her good intentions, her thoughts returned to him constantly—relentlessly.

He'd said he was catching a plane, but not whether his trip was business or pleasure. And for a moment she had an image of the leggy brunette he'd dined with at Mignonette. Would she be in the adjoining seat on the aircraft? Sharing his bed tonight in some foreign hotel?

She realised she was twisting the silk as if it was a throat, and paused, controlling her flurried breathing with an effort.

Flying could be dangerous, she told herself as she cleared the kitchen. Even before the threat of hijacking and terrorist attack, planes had been known to crash.

He could be killed, she thought with piercing desolation, and no one would bring me the news, or even acknowledge it had happened. Because there's probably nobody in his life who knows that I exist. And for all I know his name might not even be Liam. And he doesn't have to be dead.

All he need do is go—and not come back.

I would just be left feeling this appalling—eternal—emptiness, without hope or respite.

She knelt on the floor beside the empty refrigerator, resting her forehead against the chill of its door as she realised, shocked, what she had just allowed herself to admit.

How can I be so sure of this? she asked herself numbly. How can I possibly have come so far, and so quickly, when it's the last thing on earth I ever wanted to happen? When it's what I've been fighting against, for heaven's sake.

She gave a small, broken sigh, then got slowly to her feet.

Liam, she thought wretchedly, is not the only one with secrets. Not any more. But mine are going to be so much harder to keep.

Oh, God, I shall have to be so careful—so very careful.

CHAPTER EIGHT

NEARLY a week, Cat thought, her heart lurching painfully, and still not a word from Liam.

I'll be in touch, he'd said. But he'd made no promises about how soon the contact might be, and the need to see him again, to hear his voice and to touch him, was becoming well-nigh unbearable.

In working hours she was smiling, efficient, and determinedly busy. Even a little driven. If she could have stayed in the office twenty-four hours a day, she'd have been fine, she told herself wryly.

But at home, in the evenings, her comfortable flat became a cage, where she paced restlessly up and down, cooked meals she did not want, read books she did not remember, and watched television programmes she did not see. She was plagued continually by the idea that he'd had second thoughts about their arrangement and decided to abandon it. That one night she'd find a note pushed under her door, telling her so.

She was half tempted to go round to the flat to see if it was still set up in readiness for them, but the possibility of finding it stripped and empty held her in check. She would rather go on hoping, she thought, even when all hope was gone. And she hadn't reached that point yet.

At other times she wondered if he was keeping her waiting deliberately, bringing her anticipation of their next encounter to a fever pitch. If so, his plan was working brilliantly, she told herself bitterly.

Even with only her memories of his lovemaking to sustain her she was in turmoil, her senses heightened almost to screaming point.

And now here it was, Friday evening, and she had the bottomless pit of the weekend gaping in front of her again. And how pathetic was that? Putting her life on hold, just in case she was summoned.

There were several other options available to her, of course, she thought, frowning. Her father and mother were still in London, after all, and it was time she saw something of them both. Or she could pay her aunt Susan a long overdue visit.

But when she rang the number it was Belinda who answered the phone. 'Oh, it's you,' she said flatly. 'Did you want something in particular?'

'I thought your mother might like some company,' Cat said. 'I hadn't realised you were back from your honeymoon.'

'Well, you know now.' Belinda hesitated. 'And Tony's spending the weekend here too. I gather he's feeling a bit raw about you, so I don't suggest you join us.'

Cat controlled herself with an effort. She said quietly, 'Thanks for telling me,' and rang off.

She had no better luck at the Savoy. 'Miss Carlton is away for the weekend, madam. May we give her a message on her return?'

And the answer-machine was switched on at her father's Kensington flat.

'Hi, Dad,' she said, remembering too late that he preferred her to call him David. 'Just touching base. Call me some time.'

She changed into jeans and tee shirt, and began some determined flat-cleaning. She had just sunk down on the sofa, with a cup of coffee, to admire her shining domain, when there was a brisk knock on the door.

Cat started violently, spilling some of the coffee on to her newly vacuumed rug, then crossed the room, her heart thudding, and threw the door wide.

'So there you are, my pet.' Her father's tone was breezy as he strode in. 'I got your message.' He kissed her on both cheeks, then held her at arms' length to examine her critically.

'Hmm—a little pale for midsummer. You look as if you could do with a break.'

'Well, all holiday plans are on hold.' Cat forced a smile, hating herself for feeling disappointed. 'I—I'm too busy at work just now.'

'But all alone on Friday evening?' David Adamson clicked his tongue reprovingly. 'That won't do, sweetheart.'

'I'm fine.' Cat looked past him, but there was no sign of Sharine. 'Anyway, you seem to be on your own, too.'

'Temporarily,' her father returned airily. 'I'm treating Sharine to a few days at a health farm.'

'Oh.' Cat digested this. 'Is she feeling off-colour?'

'We've been up in Scotland for the past week, and it rained every day. She was not impressed.' There was a faint dryness in his tone. 'Have you eaten?' He handed her a bulging carrier bag. 'I stopped off at the deli round the corner. There's chicken Caesar salad, bread, cheese and a peach tart. Oh, and a bottle of Pouilly Fumé.'

'Wonderful.' Cat took the bag into the kitchen and began to unpack it. David followed her in, pouring himself a beaker of coffee and leaning against the sink.

'So why were you in Scotland?' she asked. 'You surely haven't taken up golf—or fishing?'

'God forbid.' David gave a smile of pure satisfaction. 'I've been staying with Nevil Beverley and his wife. He's just finishing his new play, and I'm to play the lead. That's really why I returned from California.' He lowered his voice confidentially. 'I'm going back into the theatre, and Oliver Ingham is directing me. He was staying with Nevil too, and we thrashed the whole thing out.'

Cat's brows rose. 'Really?' She shook her head. 'I thought you were totally dedicated to films.'

'I was.' Her father shrugged. 'But it's good to rethink—change directions occasionally.'

'Yes,' Cat said slowly. 'I suppose it is.' *If it's not too late,* she thought, and bit back a sigh.

'So, what's the play about?' she enquired, as they were eating. 'I presume it's a comedy?'

'Shakespeare.' David drank some wine. 'He's enjoying success as a playwright, and he's fallen in love with Mary Fitton, who was one of Queen Elizabeth's maids of honour, and possibly the Dark Lady of the sonnets as well. He has to go back to Stratford to tell his wife Anne Hathaway that their marriage is over.'

He leaned back in his chair. 'But she has other ideas, and he finds it harder to tear himself away than he thought. And then Mary Fitton comes to find him and take him back to London. And they fight for his heart and soul.'

'Which Mary Fitton wins, presumably?'

'Neither of them win.' David smiled at her. 'Because they both realise that his only real love is the theatre.' He shook his head. 'It's a wonderful script, full of poetry and emotion. I can't wait to start rehearsals.'

Cat took some more salad. 'So Sharine will be going back to America?'

'On the contrary.' David studiously avoided her gaze. 'She's going to play Mary Fitton.'

Cat put her fork down. 'The Dark Lady?' she asked incredulously. 'Can she act?'

'Of course,' David said stiffly. 'She has real talent. She read for Oliver and he was most impressed. She'll wear a wig, naturally, but that's no problem.'

'None at all,' Cat agreed drily. *Just as long as you're not planning to cast her as my stepmother as well,* she thought, with an inward grimace. She paused. 'And who's playing Anne Hathaway?'

'Not decided yet.' David refilled their glasses. 'Oliver has a few actresses in mind.' He looked at her, frowning faintly. 'So you'll be seeing much more of me from now on.' He hesitated. 'The prospect doesn't seem to have you jumping for joy.'

'I'm very pleased,' Cat said steadily. 'I just have a lot of other things on my mind.'

David seemed in no hurry to leave. He clearly wanted to talk about the play, and Cat brewed more coffee and listened, wondering, as she did so, what her mother's reaction would be to the news.

But I have enough problems of my own, she thought soberly, after he'd eventually gone. I can't worry about two people who don't even want to be in the same room with each other. And she sighed.

She was just finishing breakfast the next morning when she heard the doorbell. She went slowly to answer it, bracing herself for more disappointment.

It was the same courier standing outside, but this time he was holding a bouquet of flowers—pink, deeply scented roses and freesias. He handed her the card in its tiny envelope.

'I've been told to wait for a reply, madam.'

The card said simply, 'Tomorrow night—please?'

She buried her face in the flowers, inhaling their fragrance. Her voice was husky. 'The message is—that—that will be fine.'

The door closed and she stood for a moment, her eyes closed. She thought, Tomorrow night. Then repeated it aloud, over and over again, her voice high with laughter as she danced round her living room, with Liam's flowers held close against her breasts.

It seemed to Cat that Sunday night would never come. She'd spent most of Saturday morning going through her wardrobe and deciding that most of the things in it were boring, especially her underwear drawer. During the afternoon she'd gone shopping for replacements, choosing pretty lacy things in pastel colours rather than the overtly sexy gear that most of the boutiques were offering.

On Sunday she went for a walk in the park, lunched at a

bistro near her flat, and tried and failed to read the newspapers. She applied a face pack, and took a long and leisurely bath, then gave herself a manicure.

She was wildly, stingingly nervous as she began to pack her overnight bag. Liam hadn't mentioned a time, but she wanted to be ready when the car came for her.

I don't want to waste a minute of my time with him, she told herself.

She chose one of her new bra and brief sets in white broderie anglaise, topping them with a linen shift dress in a soft, deep blue. She was just fastening the zip when the knock on the door came.

'I'm coming,' she called, as she dealt with the safety chain and undid the latch. Only to find herself confronted by her mother.

'Hello, darling.' Vanessa Carlton sauntered in, unfastening the jacket of her pale primrose suit. 'They gave me your message at the hotel, so I thought I'd come round and see you. Spend a nice girlie evening together. Did you want anything special?'

'Well, no.' Cat swallowed her dismay. 'It was just that I hadn't seen you for a while and...'

'Well, you'll be seeing much more of me from now on.' Vanessa disposed herself elegantly on the sofa. 'If you've any Chardonnay in the fridge, I'd like some,' she added.

'Yes,' Cat said mechanically. 'Yes, of course.' Oh, God, she wailed inwardly, as she found the corkscrew and opened the bottle. This is a disaster.

'Could you manage to take a few hours off early next week?' Vanessa asked, taking the glass Cat was proffering. 'I'd really like you to come flat-hunting with me.'

'Flat-hunting?' Cat nearly spilled her own wine down the blue dress. 'You can't be tired of the Savoy, surely?'

'No, but I don't want to take up permanent residence either.'

'But I thought you'd be going back to Beverly Hills?'

'Well, normally I would be,' Vanessa said. 'But London's an interesting place at the moment. There are a couple of projects I'm looking at, so I've decided to stay where the work is.' She lifted her glass, an odd smile playing round her lips. 'Cheers, darling.'

'And what about Gil? His work's in America, isn't it? He won't want to stay here.'

'Ah, Gil,' Vanessa said meditatively. 'Let's just say that negotiations are in progress.'

She leaned back against the cushions and looked her daughter up and down, her smile widening.

'You look very nice, Cathy. That's a good colour for you.' She glanced at her watch. 'Would you like to go and eat somewhere?'

Cat nerved herself. 'Actually, I can't,' she said. 'I'm going out already—to see friends.'

'And taking an overnight bag, I see.' Vanessa missed nothing. 'These people must be incredibly—friendly.' She paused expectantly. 'So tell me, sweetie, are you embarking on a private life at last? And, if so, who is he?'

'If I told you,' Cat said steadily, 'it would no longer be private.' *And how can I tell you what I don't even know myself?*

'Wow.' Vanessa lifted her eyebrows. 'If you want to hug it to yourself as a closely guarded secret it must be important.' She paused. 'As a concerned mother, don't I get even a teensy clue?'

Cat gave her an ironic look. 'Is that how you see yourself?'

Vanessa was unoffended. 'Let's just say it's a new role that I'm considering—among others.'

As the door sounded she gave Cat a triumphant look. 'And I think your secret life just hit the dust, my sweet.'

The driver was waiting impassively outside.

'I'm sorry, but I have an unexpected visitor,' Cat apologised in a low voice. 'I'll get a cab as soon as she's gone.'

'I have my instructions, madam.' His smile was polite.

'And no other appointments, so there's no hurry. Whenever you're ready.'

Cat turned back into the room to find Vanessa standing at the window.

'Nice car, darling. Is that what Cinderella's coach looks like these days? No sign of Prince Charming unfortunately,' she added, moving back to the sofa and refilling her glass. 'I shall just have to live in hope.' And she sat down, crossing her legs with a seraphic smile.

Cat bit her lip. 'Mother, the driver's waiting for me. I—I really need to go.'

Vanessa tutted. 'Piece of maternal advice, my pet. Don't seem too eager.'

'Treat 'em mean, keep 'em keen?' Cat queried coolly. 'Isn't that a little dated?'

Her mother laughed. 'Don't you believe it. So, just relax and drink your wine, while we work out a day for flat-hunting. I'm quite serious about this.'

She was quite serious about a number of things, Cat thought resignedly as she sat down and reached for her glass.

She said, 'The hotel said you'd gone away for the weekend. Was it anywhere special?'

Vanessa shrugged. 'A get-together with old friends. I had a wonderful time.'

'Did you take your—Gil?'

'He had people of his own to see.' Vanessa gave her an amused glance. 'We're not joined at the hip, you know.'

She began to chat inconsequentially about a fashion show she'd attended, an exhibition opening soon at the National Gallery, a play she'd seen, long past its shelf-life.

It was all light-hearted stuff, faintly spiced with malice, and at any other time Cat would have sat back and enjoyed the performance. But not now. As the time relentlessly approached the hour she was on tenterhooks, in case Liam grew tired of waiting for her.

And when her mother finally put down her glass, and

reached a leisurely hand for her bag, Cat could have shouted aloud in relief.

'So why don't you come to the Savoy on Tuesday morning?' Vanessa suggested as they walked to the door. 'We can go and look at the flats the agents have found for me, and then have lunch at Vanni's.'

Cat had been working a lot of extra hours lately. Andrew was not likely to object to her having some time off, she thought.

'Fine,' she agreed. 'Shall we say around ten?'

'Well, certainly not before,' Vanessa said with a touch of acerbity, then paused. 'I suppose cabs are the usual nightmare round here? Perhaps your driver would take me on to the hotel after he's dropped you at your assignation,' she added innocently.

Nice try, Ma, thought Cat. 'I think he'd find it easier to go via the Savoy,' she returned evenly, catching a glimpse of chagrin in her mother's eyes. 'Otherwise, no problem.'

Except that it meant she was going to be later than ever, she realised, as, with Vanessa duly delivered, the car threaded its way back through the evening traffic in the West End.

The flat was quiet when she let herself in, but she could see a narrow ribbon of light under the sitting room door. So he had waited after all, she thought, her heart leaping.

She was rehearsing her apology as she opened the door and went in, then paused, the words dying on her lips.

Liam was lying back in the corner of the sofa, one arm thrown along the top of the cushions, eyes closed, his breathing soft and regular, so fast asleep that he didn't stir as she shut the door behind her, or even when she said his name. Twice.

His jacket was on the floor, along with his tie, and the top buttons of his shirt were undone. He looked comfortable and extremely peaceful, she decided as she took her case through to the bedroom. But it wasn't the reception she'd expected by any means.

When she returned, he still hadn't stirred. Cat stood watching him for a moment, then kicked off her shoes and curled up beside him, resting her cheek against his chest, breathing the unique male scent of him.

He murmured something indistinguishable and his arm encircled her shoulders, drawing her nearer. She responded instantly, nestling closer and sliding her hand inside his shirt, relishing the warm, smooth texture of his skin under her palm and the deep, steady beat of his heart.

She would let him go on sleeping for a little while, she thought, and then she would kiss him awake, so that their time together could begin. But for the moment she felt curiously, almost luxuriously content. And even a little drowsy herself.

Which was ridiculous, of course, she told herself firmly, and closed her eyes.

When she opened them again, the first thing she saw was the bedroom window, with sunlight seeping through the curtains. The next was her blue dress, draped over a chair.

And the third was Liam, beside her in the bed, propped up on one elbow as he watched her.

He said, 'Good morning,' and there was amusement in his voice. 'I was jet-lagged. What's your excuse?'

Cat shook her head. 'I don't understand. What happened?'

'I woke up on the sofa, around two a.m., and found you in my arms, dead to the world. So I carried you in here, and put you to bed.'

She stared at him. 'You took my dress off—and I slept through it? How did you manage that?'

His faint smile became a wicked grin. 'Years of practice, darling,' he drawled, and moved with the speed of light to grab the pillow from her hand before she could hit him with it.

'Actually, I think you'd have slept through the Last Trumpet,' he went on, drawing her into his arms. 'Whereas I was unusually restless, having seen those lacy scraps under your dress. But I didn't trust myself to dispose of them as well.'

Cat smiled against his shoulder. 'I'm glad they weren't completely wasted.' She pressed her lips to his skin and began to move down his body, feathering a trail of soft, beguiling kisses. 'Maybe we could still make use of them.'

Liam halted her with a groan of regret. 'Darling, we can't. Have you seen the time? I have early meetings.'

'Hell.' Cat gave her watch a despairing glance. 'I should be out of here too. Oh, I can't bear it.'

Liam bent his head, kissing her mouth with rueful hunger. 'Would it break any rules if we met again tonight?' he murmured. 'I promise to stay awake this time.'

'I'd love to,' Cat whispered back. 'But only if you also promise to stay all night.'

'Agreed.' He kissed her again. 'But on one condition. That you bring an alarm clock.'

Cat lay watching him search for his clothes, nerving herself. At last she said, 'Talking of rules…'

'Mmm?' He was buttoning his shirt, but he shot her a lightning glance.

'I don't really need a car and a chauffeur to get me here,' she said. 'I can make it on my own.'

'He'll be here for you shortly,' he said. 'But it can be the last time, if that's what you want.'

'Please.' She paused. 'Also, I got held up last night, and there was no way to warn you. So—maybe—it would be sensible to exchange mobile phone numbers—for emergencies.'

Liam looked at her, brows raised. 'I thought that was exactly what you didn't want?'

She hunched a shoulder. 'We're both busy people, and—things happen. I don't want any misunderstandings either. Numbers only,' she added hastily. 'No other details, of course.'

'Naturally.' There was a note of irony in his voice. 'And emergencies only. Then let's do it.'

Cat was thoughtful when he'd gone. It had hardly been an eager concession on his part. It seemed that he'd really bought into the idea of separate lives.

But then, so have I, she reminded herself. I didn't ask what had caused his jet-lag. He didn't ask why I was late. And that's a kind of trust—isn't it?

How will I ever know? she thought. And sighed.

She had just come out of a meeting, and was returning to her desk via the coffee machine, when her mobile phone rang.

She looked at the screen with a kind of stunned disbelief as she answered.

'Liam—has something happened?' She swallowed. 'Can't you make it this evening after all?'

'Nothing like that. I just needed to hear your voice.'

She realised she was smiling absurdly, her face warming. She tried to sound severe. 'That's hardly an emergency.'

'You have your definition,' he said softly. 'I have mine. And I want you to know I'm counting the hours until tonight.'

'Me too.' Her voice was husky, shaking a little.

After they'd disconnected, she sat staring at the little electronic miracle in her hand. My lifeline, she thought, to him. And he'd called her.

'You're very cheerful this morning,' Megs commented on her way past. 'You must be on a promise.'

Cat returned a dutiful smile as she slipped her phone back into her bag.

How wrong can you be? she thought, dragging herself back down to earth with painful effort. There were no promises—no commitment. Just this one tenuous and strictly temporary link.

So I'll have to make the most of it, she told herself soberly. For as long as it lasts.

CHAPTER NINE

'REALLY, darling,' said Vanessa. 'You're being no help at all.'

Cat, still lost in the blissful euphoria of the previous night, gave a slight start, and hurriedly reminded herself why she was there.

'What's the matter?' Vanessa went on, giving her a shrewd look. 'Doing a little nest-building on your own account?'

Cat bit her lip. 'Please don't be absurd. I have somewhere to live, if you remember.'

'A bachelor girl's pad,' her mother said with a sniff. 'I hoped you might be broadening your horizons.'

'My horizons are just fine, thanks. Regarding what we've seen so far...' She paused as the waiter brought their desserts. 'I liked the little house in Chelsea best. And Holland Park wasn't bad either.'

'Bad vibes, sweetie.' Vanessa shook her head. 'I don't think the previous tenants were very happy.'

'Anyway,' Cat went on, 'shouldn't you be asking Gil what he thinks rather than me?'

Vanessa shrugged. 'He'll go along with whatever I decide. And you seem very concerned for his feelings all of a sudden,' she added. 'You're not becoming fixated on him, I hope, because it wouldn't do you much good.'

'Not at all,' Cat said crisply. 'I just find it odd you haven't consulted him.'

'Well, don't worry about it, darling. Gil and I understand each other very well, believe me.' Her mother paused. 'And you're right; it will have to be Chelsea. Such a pretty garden, and the right atmosphere, too.' She sighed contentedly. 'That's so important for me, particularly now.'

Cat observed her with narrowed eyes. 'Why now?' she enquired. 'And also, why the rush? Mother—what are you up to?'

Vanessa spread her hands. 'Darling—I've always needed absolute peace when I'm studying a part. You know that.'

'Is that why the house in Beverly Hills was always teeming with people?' Cat asked drily.

'But I was filming then.' Vanessa's eyes were limpid. 'Live theatre is entirely different.'

Cat put down her dessert fork and sat forward. 'You're—going into a play?' she said slowly. 'When did you decide this?'

Vanessa inspected a minute fleck on her nail. 'When adorable Oliver Ingham offered me the role of Anne Hathaway in his new production,' she said lightly. 'I went up to Scotland at the weekend to discuss it with him and agree terms. Nevil Beverley wrote the script, and, believe me, sweetie, it's to die for.'

'So I've heard,' Cat said grimly. 'And death could well be involved.' She paused. 'You do know, I suppose, that my father's playing opposite you as Will Shakespeare?'

'Well, they were bound to mention it,' said Vanessa. 'And I think if Oliver can cure him of some of those tiresome mannerisms he might be quite good.' She smiled reminiscently. 'In fact, it could be quite like old times.'

'Oh, God,' Cat said weakly. She looked her mother in the eye. 'Are you completely crazy—going into a production with David and his girlfriend? It'll be a nightmare. You must see that. Why, you don't even speak.'

'Well, neither did Shakespeare and Anne Hathaway for most of the time, so the story already calls for a certain amount of tension.' Vanessa purred. 'I feel it could be quite a challenge—for all of us, especially the little American. Such a change from pantyhose commercials.'

She put her napkin on the table and rose. 'Now, order us both some coffee, darling, while I go to the powder room.'

And she departed, amid a flurry of excited whispers from neighbouring tables, leaving a troubled Cat staring after her.

Whether she liked it or not, there were clearly stormy times ahead, she thought as she signalled to the waiter.

There was no chance, of course, that her father would pull out of the production. He would regard that as a serious defeat in the ongoing post-marital war with his ex-wife. No, he would do it if it killed him.

And the press, of course, would have a field day. David Adamson and Vanessa Carlton starring together in the West End for the first time since their very public divorce. There would be vultures gathering from all directions, awaiting the latest furore. Plenty of rats in the arras to cover the inevitable spats during rehearsal. She could see the headlines now.

But David and Vanessa were actors, she told herself with an inward shrug. They thrived on publicity, whatever form it took.

Her main concern would be to avoid getting caught in the power struggle between them. Which meant extending her policy of non-involvement somehow.

And that reminded her of another, quite different problem. Because this property hunt had turned out to be seriously bad news, she told herself grimly. Galling as it might be, Vanessa had not been far out in her comment about nest-building.

Cat reluctantly admitted to herself that she'd been viewing the flats and houses on offer totally through her own eyes, having all kinds of illicit daydreams about moving into them with Liam. In her mind, she'd filled each space with furniture that they'd chosen together. Picked the room where they would spend every night in each other's arms. Imagined how their life might be together.

And there was no point in that kind of thinking, she chastised herself vehemently. Because it was not only stupid, but dangerous. And also totally out of character.

I must have been led astray by last night, she thought wryly.

Which turned out to be the stuff that dreams are made on. And the breath caught in her throat as she remembered...

She'd arrived to find Liam already waiting for her, his hunger and impatience undisguised and unashamed as she walked straight into his arms, her lips parting under his, her body already on fire for him.

There had not even been time to draw breath, let alone undress. He had drawn her down with him onto the heavy rug in front of the fire, freeing himself from his clothing and tearing her underwear aside before taking her with stark, passionate urgency.

It had been harsh, glorious, and over much too soon, her body driven to climax with a fierce absorption that had matched his own.

Afterwards they had lain together, shaken by the power of their mutual consummation, caught between laughter and tears. And later Liam had taken her to the bedroom, where he'd removed her clothes, slowly and gently, between kisses, and made love to her again with exquisite, almost languid restraint, tempting her, leading her on with the promise of release, until a voice she'd hardly recognised as her own had whimpered in pleading for the long withheld fulfilment, all remaining inhibitions lost.

Sheer exhaustion had impelled them to sleep at last, but at dawn Cat had been woken once more by his hands on her body, turning to him warmly, eagerly, offering herself to his caresses and all that would follow, her senses already anticipating the peak of rapture.

It had been the most wonderful night of her life, she thought, her body shivering in swift delight, but it had done nothing to ease the inevitable morning parting from him.

She had not expected, she realised with bewilderment, to need him so much, in so many ways that transcended simple desire. Against her will, her feelings were becoming more complex—and more disturbing. And that was where the real peril lay.

Because she had no idea what Liam felt in return, if anything. Oh, he enjoyed her. There was no doubting that. He seemed to derive the same incredible pleasure from her body as he gave.

But he seemed to accept completely the strict limitations that she'd imposed on their relationship, and gave no hint that he wanted more than the fevered delight of physical union with her.

And it was these limitations that she was beginning to find so irksome. Because each time she saw him she found more and more that she wanted to share other things with him as well. She wanted to tell him about her job, and ask about how he spent his working day.

She'd been aware from the first of the dynamic, restless energy he concealed under his laid-back manner. Only when he was asleep was it ever wholly subdued. He looked younger then, too, and Cat thought she sometimes detected a trace of vulnerability. But that might be wishful thinking. Another vain attempt to figure him out.

His life was clearly hectic. He was either flying off somewhere, or going from meeting to meeting. Money was clearly not a problem either, she told herself wryly. He wore expensive clothes, and he still refused point-blank to let her contribute towards the running expenses of the flat they were sharing.

She was curious, also, about his family. Was he an only child, or were there siblings? Were his parents still alive?

There was so much about him she didn't know—and might never find out, Cat thought, biting her lip.

And at the present time it would have been good to confide in him about David and Vanessa, and this witch's brew of trouble they were concocting between them, but, like all personal topics, this was out of bounds.

Most of all, she missed the ordinary things—the preparation of a meal, the enjoyment of a television programme, even the right to sleep with him each night and wake in his arms every morning.

And if he found sex an adequate substitute for all these other, deeper intimacies, then she did not.

Cat sighed under her breath. She had not easily accepted this sudden change of heart, especially when she'd been so adamant about the terms of their affair. Nor could she explain it, either, to her own satisfaction.

And she could never, ever tell Liam.

She had no illusions about it. If he had even an inkling of the thoughts running through her mind as she'd followed her mother from one desirable residence to another this morning, then she would probably never see him again. A notion she frankly found completely unbearable, she thought, her throat tightening.

The waiter arrived with the coffee, and she looked up with a brief smile to thank him, and saw, over his shoulder, Liam entering the restaurant with two other men.

For a stunned, shaken moment she thought she was hallucinating—that he was just a figment of her imagination, conjured up from her emotional depths because he'd been at the forefront of her mind.

Then she realised that the restaurant manager, all smiles, was advancing to greet the new arrivals and conduct them to a table on the other side of the room.

Oh, God, she thought, the pulse pounding in her throat. First Mignonette—now here. It can't be possible. Lightning doesn't strike twice—does it?

Yet why shouldn't Liam be here? It was another 'in' place—the kind of establishment that seemed his natural habitat. And at least he was in male company this time. There was no smart brunette with legs up to her armpits.

All the same, she told herself almost frantically, I didn't expect this. I can't handle it.

She would have hidden behind the menu, but the waiter had cleared it from the table, and, as Liam turned to follow

his companions, he saw her. The cheerful lunchtime hubbub
in the restaurant seemed to fade into silence as his gaze locked
with hers. His expression mirrored her surprise, but there was
amusement in his face, and delight too as he looked at her.

Then, pausing only for a swift word with the others, he
started towards her, threading his way purposefully between
the tables.

And from the other direction came Vanessa, smiling radi-
antly as she acknowledged the greetings from other customers
as if she was on some royal progress.

She reached the table first. 'Aren't people really sweet?'
she said, resuming her seat and pouring herself some coffee.
'A woman over there told me she'd seen me opposite your
father in *The Taming of the Shrew* at Stratford all those years
ago. That was when I found out I was having you, of course,
and by the end of the run they'd had to let out all my dresses.'
She pulled a face. 'I don't think the wardrobe mistress ever
forgave me.'

Cat was on her feet, grabbing for her bag. She said, 'May
we go, please? I should be back at work.'

'Already?' Vanessa looked at her watch. 'But we haven't
had our coffee yet. And, anyway, I thought you'd come with
me—take another look at the Chelsea house.'

'I'm sorry, I can't.' She felt as if she was gasping for air.
'I'll get the bill...' She turned to leave, but her path was
already blocked.

'Miss Adamson?' Liam said softly. 'It is Miss Adamson,
isn't it?' There was open challenge in his gaze, and the be-
ginnings of anger too. 'What a charming surprise.'

He turned to Vanessa. 'And Miss Carlton.' He shook his
head. 'This is a real privilege. I must be your greatest fan.'

'How dear of you to say so.' Vanessa's eyes flickered over
him in swift assessment and she allowed her smile to widen—
approvingly and invitingly. The way Cat had seen it happen
so many times before when attractive men appeared in her
orbit.

But never when it's been my man, she thought. Not until now.

Her mother held out her hand, and Liam bent his head and dropped a light kiss on it. It was an overt homage to a beautiful woman, carried out with charm, and Vanessa clearly revelled in it.

'So,' she said, 'how do you know my little Catherine?'

Liam straightened. He was smiling, but the eyes that rested on Cat were cold. 'Miss Adamson and I have met once or twice,' he said. 'On business. But perhaps she doesn't remember.'

A pit of ice seemed to be opening up inside her. She said, her face wintry, 'Of course I remember. But now business calls me away again, I'm afraid.'

'I hope,' Liam said, too courteously, 'that you're not leaving on my account.'

Her mouth was dry. 'I—just have to go.' She turned again to Vanessa. 'Are you coming? Can I get you a taxi?'

'No, thank you, my pet.' Vanessa leaned back in her chair. 'She's so impatient,' she told Liam. 'But I am equally determined to stay here and finish my coffee.' She paused. 'Are people waiting for you, or can you keep me company for a while?'

'I'd be honoured,' he said, and took Cat's vacated chair. He didn't look up at her as she mumbled goodbye, and she got only a vague, sweet smile from her mother as she bent and gave her an awkward peck on the cheek.

Vanessa, she realised as she made her way to the cashier's desk, had already moved on. And it was really quite funny, except that she didn't feel like laughing.

My name, she thought. All this time he's known my name and said nothing. But how? She swallowed. She knew the answer to that, of course, and cursed all the easily charmed receptionists at Anscote Manor.

Not that she could altogether blame them. Even without trying, Liam exerted a powerful sexual charisma. Something

Vanessa, a fellow predator, had sensed immediately and responded to.

I've no doubt she's found out who he is by now, she thought, gritting her teeth. She probably has his entire history, down to his inside leg measurement.

I must remember to ask next time I see her—*Mother, what's the name of the man I'm sleeping with?*

'Is everything all right, madam?'

Cat realised the cashier was looking at her with faint concern, and hurriedly composed her face. 'Everything's fine,' she said. 'And the food was superb.'

As she left, she risked a last look back, and instantly regretted it. Because they were still together, talking quietly. Liam had even moved his chair closer to hers, and Vanessa was smiling into his eyes, one hand on the sleeve of his jacket.

Cat's hand clenched painfully round the strap of her bag, and she hurried, head down, out into the sunlight.

I've been defeated, she told herself. In a battle I didn't even know had begun.

Andrew had given her the whole day off, but she had every intention of going back to work for the afternoon. Yet somehow she found herself asking the cab-driver to take her to Wynsbroke Gardens instead.

She badly needed to be alone, and she could think of nowhere else.

But it was far from ideal as a sanctuary, as Cat discovered when, instead of the silence she craved, she found memories assailing her from every direction as soon as she walked in.

Liam's voice murmuring to her, the tremble of their breathing, the caress of his naked skin against hers—she was aware of it everywhere.

She sank down on the sofa, closing her eyes and putting her hands over her ears, trying to block it out.

Because now there were other images and other memories and she had to deal with them.

So, she thought painfully, that was Liam—the real one. Only twelve hours ago she'd been wrapped in his arms, feeling totally secure. Unutterably safe. Now she was alone on the mountainside and the wind was cold.

She had to accept that he was the same as any other man— easily bored with the status quo, always on the prowl, eternally seeking diversion. Treating faith and trust like dirty words. Everything she'd always dreaded. Everything she'd tried to protect herself from.

I actually let myself think for a while he might be different, she whispered silently. God knows, I so *wanted* him to be different, even though he had 'heartbreak' written all over him. What a fool I've been. But at least he never knew that...

There was a bottle of armagnac on the little sideboard, and she poured some into a balloon glass before returning to sit down again.

She'd had to watch the 'Vanessa effect', as her father had once wryly called it, pretty much all her life. Her mother wasn't just a strikingly beautiful, instinctively sensuous woman. She had real star quality. If she was in a room no one ignored her, unless she so chose. On stage or film set, it took a formidable performer to stand up against her.

So it should have come as no surprise that Liam had been instantly enthralled by her. And, knowing that, why did she feel this agony of shock and betrayal?

After all, she had no claim on Liam. She had insisted on that. He was a free agent, under the terms of their deal, and so was she. And, as Gil no longer seemed to be a major player, Vanessa was presumably free to choose also. And she clearly had her sights set on Liam.

Another one to add to her list of toyboys...

Cat sank her teeth into her lower lip until she tasted blood. Because it didn't have to be like this, she thought. And it shouldn't have been. It was all her own fault.

If it hadn't been for this ridiculous, nauseating sex-without-commitment demand of hers, she could have met Liam openly, and arranged to introduce her mother to him in perfect safety. Because if Vanessa had known that Liam belonged to her daughter it was probable she'd have subdued the dazzle, and deliberately downplayed the role of *femme fatale*. She'd done it before when it hadn't really mattered.

And, to give her credit, she had no idea it mattered now. She'd simply obeyed her instincts, and attracting men was like a conditioned reflex for her. She was Vanessa Carlton, and ordinary rules did not apply.

Cat kicked off her shoes and curled up on the sofa, folding her arms across her body like a barricade. But it was too late for that. Her defences were already down, and the hurt could be mortal.

She couldn't even adopt the moral high ground and tell herself how disgusting it was that her mother should set out to ensnare another man so many years younger than herself, because it simply wasn't true. By no stretch of the imagination was Vanessa old enough to be his mother.

She was still under forty-five, and Liam was almost certainly in his early thirties. Cat would be surprised if there was more than twelve years between them. And successful relationships were constantly being launched on much greater age differences than that, she admitted painfully.

But this—*this*—was something she definitely had not foreseen.

She heard a sound from downstairs—like a door closing—and stiffened, putting down her glass.

The flat was in its usual pristine condition, so the cleaners had already been. Which didn't leave many other options.

It had to be Liam's footsteps she could hear on the stairs—but had he come alone?

It was his flat, she told herself, her throat tightening convulsively. He paid the rent. He had the right to do as he wished—to bring any visitors he wanted. For all she knew he might have been having other assignations there all along.

By the time he came into the room she was on her feet, staring towards the door.

He seemed to be alone, and her heart contracted in almost shameful relief.

He halted, looking back at her, his face expressionless. 'Is the place haunted?'

'Haunted?' she echoed in bewilderment. It was the last thing she'd expected him to say, and it threw her. 'What do you mean?'

'You look,' he said, 'as if you've seen a ghost.'

Cat lifted her chin. 'I wasn't expecting any interruptions,' she said shortly. 'What are you doing here?'

'I came to find you,' he said slowly. 'You weren't at your own place, so I guessed you might be here.'

She swallowed. 'And where is Vanessa?'

He shrugged. 'Paying another visit to some place in Chelsea, I believe. You should know better than I. You're her daughter, after all.'

'Did she tell you that?'

'I think she was tempted by godchild,' he said reflectively. 'But the fact you're called Adamson rather gave the game away. As I said, I've been a fan of hers for years, and I can remember when you were born.'

He paused. 'Why do you call your mother by her given name?'

'Because she prefers it,' she said curtly.

His brows lifted. 'And what about your choice in the matter?'

'It's never made much difference to me. As it happens, I call my father David too. Not that I spend much time with either of them, of course.'

'I see,' he said.

'I'm sure you do.' She paused. 'Another piece of information to add to the file. You should have quite a dossier by now.'

He smiled faintly. 'But there are still significant gaps.'

He walked forward, and Cat found herself taking a step backwards, away from him. The edge of the sofa intervened, catching the back of her knees, and she fell untidily on to the cushions behind her.

He stopped, hands on hips, his eyes narrowing. 'What the hell's the matter with you?' he demanded harshly. 'First you cut me dead in that bloody restaurant. Now you're backing off from me. Why?'

She couldn't for the life of her think of a single reason that she was prepared to voice aloud, so she kept silent, struggling to sit up and pull her skirt straight.

'Is this your subtle way of telling me you don't want me to make love to you?' His voice was like ice. 'You thought I'd come here for a little afternoon delight? A roll in the sack to work off a late lunch? Under the circumstances, I wouldn't think that was an option.'

She said, 'I hope my presence hasn't upset any other plans you might have had.'

'I did consider getting totally blasted,' he said. 'But that would mean I'd end up with a hangover as well as a pain in the neck.' His voice bit. 'So I decided we'd have a quiet chat instead.'

'Is that really necessary?' Her own tone was mutinous. His 'pain in the neck' comment had stung.

'I think so, or I wouldn't be here.' He paused. 'So, what was all that stuff at Vanni's about? I arrive, and see the girl who woke in my arms this morning, but when I approach her I find myself being treated like a case of bubonic plague.'

'But you weren't meant to approach me,' she said. She gestured around her. 'We meet here, and only here—that's the deal. You know that.'

'I'm afraid that's no longer acceptable,' Liam said grimly. 'Unless you want me to provide a list of restaurants I plan to visit each month, so you can avoid them?'

She looked down at her hands, clasped tautly in her lap. 'No.'

'Good,' he said. 'So can we please treat any future encounters in a rather more civilised manner?'

'I suppose so,' she said. 'It was just—so unexpected.'

'And unwelcome,' he said. 'On your side, anyway.'

Cat bit her lip. She said in a low voice, 'I was embarrassed,
too. I knew that Vanessa would expect to be introduced to
you—and I don't even know your full name.'

'It's Hargrave,' he said quietly. 'Liam Hargrave—for future
reference.'

'And I wasn't sure how to explain you either.' She smiled
nervously. 'I could hardly say you were my occasional lover.'

'No,' he said. 'Probably not. How about—friend?'

'Is that what you are?'

'Yes,' he said. 'And that's a constant, whatever happens.'

He meant when their affair was over, she thought. When
his desire for her had finally faded. And it sounded awfully
like a warning—as if their days together were already num-
bered. As if…

Her mind seemed to close over. She heard herself say,
'What did you talk about with Vanessa?'

His brows lifted. 'You mean did I interrogate her about
you?' he drawled. 'Well, I might have done, given the chance,
but your mother has her own agenda, and pursues it with
remarkable single-mindedness. In which she reminds me of
you,' he added drily.

'I'm not like her. I don't want to be like her.' Her voice
was over-loud, the words sounding as if they'd been scratched
from rock, but she struggled to recover. 'Or my father, either.'

Liam moved sharply, pulling her to her feet, drawing her
into the circle of his arms and holding her, in spite of her taut
resistance.

He said, 'Tell me.'

'They didn't intend to have me,' she croaked. 'I was a
complete accident. They'd just had this fabulous breakthrough
in their careers, playing Katharine and Petruchio at Stratford,
people were lining up to hire them, and the last thing they

needed was a baby. Vanessa was talking about it over lunch—
the effect it had on the costume department,' she added with
a little choked laugh.

'But you're here,' Liam said quietly. 'So it can't have been
that much of a disaster.'

'Bad publicity.' Cat leaned her forehead against his shoulder. 'My cousin Belinda heard her talking about it once to
Aunt Susan. Vanessa had morning sickness and everyone at
the theatre knew she was pregnant. If she'd even enquired
about an abortion it would have been in all the papers the
next day. Her young goddess image would have suffered.

'So she went ahead with the pregnancy. My God, they even
called me Katharine, and people said how sweet that was.'

'Imagine if you'd been a boy,' Liam said. 'It could have
been a damned sight worse. Do you think you'd have been
Pet for short?'

'Oh, God,' she said, with a ghost of a laugh. 'I never
thought of that. Anyway, after Belinda told me, I refused to
be Katharine with a K any more. I changed to Catherine with
a C instead.'

'And to the Cat that walks by herself?'

'No.' She grimaced, shaking her head. 'That came later.'

'And what did your parents say about the change of initial?
Did they never ask why?'

'I doubt they even noticed.' She realised he was still holding her, and freed herself gently. 'My aunt and uncle brought
me up, and they were concerned, I know. But David and
Vanessa were rarely around. Besides, the marriage was just
starting to be in trouble, and they had more important consid-
erations, anyway.'

'Debatable,' he said. He paused. 'As a matter of fact, I saw
them in that production of *The Taming of the Shrew*, when I
was at school.' He shook his head. 'I thought your mother
was the most beautiful thing I'd ever seen. I even managed
to get hold of a signed photograph of her.'

'I hope you told her,' Cat said with forced lightness. 'She'd be thrilled.'

'I did,' he said. 'And she was.'

'Do you still have the photograph?'

'She asked the same thing.' He grinned slightly. 'I had to confess I wasn't sure. It was a long time ago, and I'm not much of a hoarder.'

'Well.' She smiled too. 'I dare say she'll forgive you.' She felt as if she was feeling her way round the edge of some abyss.

He shrugged. 'She seems prepared to.'

'But she doesn't know we're—involved?'

He looked past her. 'She didn't hear it from me.'

She said quietly, 'Then let's keep it like that. Stick to the rules over this at least.'

His gaze travelled slowly back to her face. 'If it's still what you want.'

'Yes, of course,' she said. 'You've accidentally met my mother, but nothing else has changed.'

Liam's mouth twisted. 'If you say so.' He paused. 'While we're on the subject, have you any other requests—or needs—that I might be able to satisfy?' He put his hands on her shoulders, drawing her towards him. 'Only because I'm here, and so are you,' he added huskily as his mouth descended towards hers. 'You do understand that, I hope?'

'But you said you weren't here for that,' Cat reminded him, her heart lurching in mingled joy and anguish.

Want me, she cried out silently. Oh, keep wanting me—please. And I'll survive on that somehow. Whatever may happen.

'I lied,' he told her softly, and began to kiss her.

CHAPTER TEN

September

CAT switched off the phone and replaced it on the table beside the bath with a deep sigh of satisfaction. Liam had been gone for nearly two weeks, and her inconsolable body had ached for him each day and night of their separation.

She lifted herself lithely out of the water and began to pat herself dry. Then she padded naked into the bedroom and removed the lid from the flat blue and gold box which waited on the bed.

The usual courier had delivered it at her own flat earlier—the latest in a series of gifts sent by Liam over the past weeks. Flowers came regularly, interspersed with delicate pieces of expensive jewellery, flasks of her favourite scent, and occasional articles of glamorous nightwear such as the present offering.

Cat caught her breath all over again as she drew the nightdress from the sheltering folds of tissue paper. The filmy white fabric seemed to drift through her hands as she held it against her. It was little more than an exquisitely simple veil for her body, with silver ribbon shoulder bows supporting a tiny bodice that barely covered her breasts, from which the skirt fell, sheer and softly revealing, to the floor. Which was exactly where it would end, once Liam had undone those pretty bows, she thought, smiling.

Her silent wish of three months ago seemed to have been granted. Liam's desire for her showed no sign of abating. Their hours together were spent in passionate abandonment to each other's pleasure.

But how he spent his time when he was not making love

to her remained a closed book. One that she wanted to open and read every page.

But that, it seemed, was not an option that would ever be available to her. She'd hoped, after the encounter with Vanessa, when he'd told her his full name, that other disclosures would naturally follow. However, there had been no breach in the wall he'd built around himself, and any tentative probing Cat had attempted had been blocked. Gently but quite firmly.

And deliberately casual remarks about new eateries she'd heard of, films she would like to see, and places she'd always meant to visit had received no response at all. As had hints that she might sometimes meet him at the airport.

When they were in bed he was a passionately generous lover, but it seemed that keeping the rest of his life a no-go area suited him very well.

She wondered sometimes what his reaction would be if she said, Hey, can we renegotiate our deal? Become a couple in public as well as private? But she did not dare, in case he turned her down. Told her, in fact, what she most dreaded to hear—that she wasn't the only lady in his life. And that someone else accompanied him to the theatre and out to dinner, and waited for his plane to land.

Because she did not think she could survive a rejection like that, or the knowledge that she wasn't the only recipient of his expertise as a lover.

However, that did not stop her looking for him, constantly and unashamedly. Every time she entered a restaurant—and she had returned several times to Mignonette and to Vanni's just to see if he was there—she was scanning the tables, half in hope, half in fear, in case he was there and not alone.

She had even scoured the telephone book for subscribers called Hargrave, and tried all those listed, but to no avail, forcing her to the conclusion that Liam protected his privacy by having an ex-directory number.

Well, she'd sold him this idea of a secret affair, however

much she might regret it now. So she had no one to blame but herself if he was better at keeping secrets than she was.

No past, not future, only the enjoyment of the present. And how could she possibly have been fool enough to make such a choice?

Because I never knew I could feel like this, she told herself, her throat tightening. And it's exactly what I was so desperate to avoid.

Liam, she had realised a long time ago, had the power to break her heart. When she had watched him with Vanessa she had been savaged by jealousy, and she was still wondering what that oddly intimate conversation had been about.

He had never referred to it since, and, more surprisingly, neither had Vanessa, although Cat had been meeting her quite regularly, and, considering her mother's reaction at her encounter with him, had expected her to mention Liam—express some opinion about him at the very least. But she'd not said a word, and Cat had decided against raising the subject herself. If Vanessa had met him and promptly forgotten him it was probably all for the best.

Besides, her mother was now deep in rehearsals for *Playwright in Residence*. Another tricky situation into which Cat had been dragged.

Her father's initial reaction to the news that his ex-wife and current mistress would soon be vying for his favours on stage had been volcanic.

'She's going to make us both a laughing stock,' he'd roared at Cat, storming up and down her sitting room. 'Why the hell didn't you talk her out of it?'

'Because it's none of my business,' Cat had retorted. 'I have my own life. You deal with it.'

By the time he'd left he'd cooled down to icy fury, and had made it clear that he'd no intention of pulling out of the production, as he'd threatened initially.

And he'd managed to deal with the resultant gleeful headlines in the press with strained good humour.

Vanessa had responded buoyantly, telling reporters it would be wonderful to work with darling David again after all this time, and offering Sharine her services as dialogue coach.

And when 'darling David' riposted by announcing that he and Sharine were engaged, Vanessa said in an interview that she could only hope with all her heart that he might somehow be able to find happiness this time.

Stalemate, Cat thought grimly, and probably worse to come.

Yet it seemed that the anticipated stand-up, knock-down rows during rehearsals had not materialised after all, and that, in spite of everything that had gone before, both her errant parents seemed to be behaving with meticulous professionalism. It was all very strange.

But no mysteries tonight, and no useless regrets either, she thought, determinedly clearing her mind. Just the continuing rapture of Liam's possession.

It seemed an eternity before she heard the downstairs door open and close.

When he came in, she was standing in the doorway of the bedroom, the lamplight behind her turning her nightgown into transparency.

For a moment he was motionless, the green eyes smoky with hunger as he looked at her.

Then he went to her, pulling her fiercely against him, his lips parting hers, draining the sweetness of her mouth with heated urgency.

'Oh, God,' he muttered unevenly, lifting his head with reluctance. 'Do you know—have you any idea how beautiful you are?'

His fingers went to the first silver bow, pulling it loose.

'Sure you're not tired after the flight?' Her voice teased and her eyes shone up at him.

'Tired is nothing.' Liam untied the second bow and watched the gown slip from her body like moonlight on a statue. His fingers were cool as they began to caress her, but they warmed and aroused everywhere he touched. And his smile was a kiss. 'With your help, my exquisite lady,' he whispered, 'I plan to be totally exhausted.'

She was dreaming, and she knew it, walking among the fallen stones of some ancient castle. Liam was ahead of her, and she had to hurry to keep up, but the path was uneven and her feet were constantly slipping, forcing her to fall behind. Making her struggle to keep him in sight. She tried to call out to him, begging him to wait, but no sound came from her throat, and when she rounded the next corner he had gone.

Cat woke gasping, reaching blindly for him, but the bed beside her was empty. She sat up, pushing her hair back from her face, looking round almost wildly, and saw him standing by the window, looking down into the communal garden below, his tall figure a deeper darkness among the shadows, and as still as one of the stones in her dream.

She stared at him, feeling oddly disturbed.

'Liam?' she said uncertainly, and he half turned. 'Liam, is something wrong?'

'Not a thing.' His voice was quiet. 'I just couldn't sleep. But I didn't mean to wake you.'

She wanted to joke that she knew the perfect cure for insomnia, but something kept her silent.

Instead, she slipped out of bed and went across to him, sliding her arms round his waist and pressing her lips to the cool nakedness of his shoulder.

She said, 'Darling, come back to bed—please.' She managed a little laugh. 'Isn't it ridiculous? I was actually having a bad dream.'

'Want to tell me?' His voice was gentle, but there was no answering smile in his eyes. He reached for his discarded shirt and draped it around her. 'Don't catch cold.'

It was much chillier tonight, she realised. The seasons were changing and summer was nearly over. She found she was shivering a little.

'There were ruins,' she said lamely. 'And I was searching for you, but I couldn't find you.'

'Well, I'm here now,' he said, stroking her hair back from her face. 'So that's all right.'

'I expect it was because I've been missing you so badly,' she said haltingly. 'It—it was a long trip.'

She found herself desperately wanting him to say, Next time I'll take you with me. And knew that it would be just the breakthrough in their relationship that she needed so badly, and that she would say yes.

But all he said was, 'Unfortunately, that can't always be helped.'

'Was I restless?' she asked, forcing down her disappointment. 'Did I disturb you? Is that why you got up?'

'I had some thinking to do,' Liam said, after a pause. 'The middle of the night can be a good time for that.'

'But not just that.' She moved closer, pressing herself against him in tacit offering, comforted by his body's immediate, instinctive response.

'No,' he said huskily. 'Not just that, my lovely witch.' And he lifted her into his arms and carried her back to the waiting bed.

Afterwards, he fell deeply asleep almost at once, but Cat stayed awake, staring into the darkness in her turn, wondering what thoughts had driven him to leave her like that. They certainly had not been happy ones, because his eyes had held an almost haunted look. And they couldn't have been about anything trivial either.

She'd sensed a change, too, in his lovemaking that last time. She'd been aware that, although the physical pleasure he gave her was as breathtakingly intense as ever, he seemed to be holding back mentally and emotionally in some strange way.

Maybe he's having business worries, she thought. Perhaps this trip hasn't gone as well as he hoped.

She had not, realistically, expected him to share his problems with her, whatever they were. After all, she still had no idea what he did for a living. But it hurt just the same to be fobbed off.

And it meant that she couldn't discuss her own anxieties with him either, even though things were tricky on the work front for her too. The troubled international situation had made people reluctant to spend money on any major changes at their premises, so the market for their services had slowed right down, and there were few new projects in the pipeline. Andrew, who usually came to work whistling, was disturbingly silent these days, and there were nasty rumours that if things didn't improve soon there might have to be some redundancies.

It could be a stormy winter, Cat thought uneasily. And she turned her head and looked at Liam's sleeping back, wishing suddenly that he would reach for her and hold her. And never let her go.

'We got the Venner contract,' said Andrew. 'Their acceptance was in this morning's mail.'

'Oh, good.' Cat, who'd been miles away, started a little. She gave him a swift glance. 'I mean, it *is* good, isn't it?'

'Anything's a bonus these days,' he said glumly. 'But it's hardly mega-stuff.'

'We've had a bad month,' Cat reminded him. 'Now it's behind us, and things will start to pick up soon.'

He grimaced. 'I hope you're right.' And he set off towards his office. 'Oh, by the way,' he added, turning back, 'have you seen today's *Clarion*? There's a piece about your mother in it.'

'No,' Cat frowned. 'What does it say?'

Andrew took the folded paper from his pocket and handed it to her. 'Read it for yourself. The gossip column.'

Cat sighed inwardly as he departed. She was still brooding

over the previous night and its aftermath, because Liam's pre-occupation had spilled over into this morning. Usually she found waking with him a wonderful experience, with laughter and tenderness tempering the ache of another separation. Often, too, Liam helped her to dress, closing zips and hooks, and refastening buttons with deft, regretful hands.

But today he'd simply showered and dressed himself, swiftly and silently. And his parting kiss had done hardly more than brush her lips.

The passionate lover who'd come back to her last night might never have existed.

There had to be something seriously on his mind, she thought. And now it was worrying her too.

I have to know, she told herself. Have to find out. But how? She'd tried ringing him, but his mobile was switched off. In fact, it was almost as if he was putting himself deliberately beyond her reach.

And the more she told herself she was imagining things, the more uneasy she became.

So the last thing she needed was Vanessa muddying the waters for her, and she sighed as she unfolded the paper and turned to the requisite page.

A special face will be missing from the first night audience when beautiful Vanessa Carlton opens in *Playwright in Residence* at the Excelsior Theatre in two weeks' time.

Ruggedly handsome boyfriend Gil Granger is on his way back to California to pursue his career in photography—and there are no plans for his return.

However, three-times married Vanessa, appropriately playing one third of a seventeenth century love triangle in Nevil Beverley's new comedy, is making a super-fast recovery from Gil's defection, and is rumoured to have his successor in place already. So, not all the drama's on the stage at the Excelsior, it seems.

And Miss Carlton's comment, when asked the identity of her new squeeze? Simply—'No comment.'

Cat put the paper down and sat staring into space. Well, she thought, it had been obvious from the start that Gil and her mother were hardly the ideal couple. But that didn't mean Vanessa would relish being dumped so publicly, and just before the play was due to open.

Damn Gil, she thought forcefully. Surely he could have hung around for another two weeks—let her get the first night over and done with.

She imagined the story of his instant replacement had probably been concocted by Vanessa herself, as a face-saving exercise. And in her place she'd probably have done the same, she admitted ruefully.

Having failed to locate her mother at the theatre, Cat dialled the number of the Chelsea house. Vanessa answered at once, sounding eager and far too cheerful for someone who'd just been jilted by a much younger man.

But her voice took a slight downturn when she realised it was Cat. 'No, darling, I'm not rehearsing this morning,' she said. 'David's blonde needs some extra work on the second act, and apparently she feels intimidated if I'm within a hundred yards of the theatre. Isn't that bizarre?'

'Amazing,' Cat agreed drily. She hesitated. 'Actually, I read the piece in the *Clarion* and I wanted to make sure you were all right—and to tell you that I'm sorry about Gil.'

'There's really no need.' Vanessa was clearly amused. 'Gil had simply outlived his usefulness, and it was time for him to go. Besides,' she added, 'he'd begun to mope quite terribly over Patric, and I was finding it all very depressing.'

'Who is Patric?' Cat queried in bewilderment.

'Gil's boyfriend, darling, an antique dealer in Santa Barbara, who loaned him to me,' Vanessa told her airily. 'After all, I was between relationships, and I could hardly come back here alone when your father was being seen everywhere with his bimbette.' She paused. 'You know, darling, I really can't do without a man to escort me, and I must say Gil did play the part of my devoted lover awfully well. Even your father was fooled. I've told Gil he should consider acting as an alternative to photography.'

She paused. 'Darling, are you still there?'

'Yes,' Cat said faintly. 'I think so. It's just that you take my breath away sometimes. How—how are you going to manage without Gil to cover for you?'

She could hear the smile in her mother's voice. 'Don't worry about that, darling. I'd never have let him leave if I didn't have other fish to fry.' Her giggle was soft and overtly sexy. 'So make sure you keep breathing, because you've seen nothing yet—believe me.' She became suddenly businesslike. 'And now I must go. My masseuse will be here at any minute.'

Cat's head was whirling as she disconnected. *Other fish to fry.* So the *Clarion* reporter had not lied, and Vanessa was involved with someone. What was more, she sounded almost gloating about it.

Suddenly, and for no particular reason, she felt afraid.

That evening, she phoned her father.

'Good God,' he said. 'To what do I owe this honour?'

'I thought maybe we could meet for a meal,' she suggested guiltily. 'Catch up on a few things. How about lunch tomorrow?'

'Dinner would be better. We're having to fit in extra rehearsals during the day.' There was a heavy note in his voice. 'Either that or delay the opening.' He paused. 'I'll get a table at Le Bonnet Rouge for eight. It will just be the two of us. Sharine will be learning her lines for act three.'

Ouch, thought Cat as she rang off. That didn't bode well for the production. But it was ideal for her own purposes. She'd met Sharine over dinner at her father's flat only once, and it had been an uphill struggle all the way. Sharine became bored easily, and showed it, and resented any conversation of which she was not the subject. Cat was wryly relieved that she would not have to spend another evening battling to be civil.

She despised herself for what she was doing, but the fear was growing inside her like a block of ice in her midriff, and there was no other way of finding out what she had to know.

She dressed carefully for the occasion, in a simple black crêpe dress, high-necked and long-sleeved, and did clever things with concealer and blusher to make it look as if she hadn't a care in the world and slept like a baby every night.

David was already waiting at the table when she arrived. He stood up and gave her an expansive hug, while the people who'd recognised him murmured to each other, 'That's his daughter.'

'You look terrific, my sweet,' he told her.

'So do you.' And she wasn't telling the truth either.

He sighed. '*Anno domini*, I'm afraid, my love.' He lowered his voice. 'I tried to grow my own beard for the part, and it was iron-grey. Quite a shock, I'll tell you.'

She sipped the dry martini he'd ordered for her and studied the menu. She said, 'Yet my mother doesn't seem to get any older—or change at all.'

His mouth tightened, but he said lightly, 'She must have a picture in the attic, like Dorian Gray.'

When they'd chosen the food she asked him about the play, and saw a shadow cross his face.

'We're at a tricky stage, but it's all going to be fine. Sharine's coming along really well now. She still has trouble with the accent, but thanks to your mother's ill-timed remarks she won't have a voice coach.' He sighed. 'She says if Gwyneth Paltrow can get away with it, so can she.'

'But she's not Gwyneth Paltrow,' Cat said drily.

'No,' David said, with a slight snap. 'She is not.' He paused. 'She doesn't like her costume either—finds the far-thingale cumbersome. She actually put in some designs of her own—the sort of thing Sophie Marceau wore in *Braveheart*—

and we had to explain that Shakespeare came three hundred years later than that. But she's still not convinced.'

Cat put up a hand to hide her quivering lips. 'Oh, Dad, I'm sorry.'

'And it doesn't help that she has this really terrific understudy,' he went on angrily. 'Your mother's suggestion, naturally. Sharine feels really undermined by it all.'

Cat picked up her fork and attacked her *coquilles Jacques*. She said in a low voice, 'Maybe she feels a bit undermined herself—with Gil going back to the States.'

'Well, I can't imagine why,' her father said tartly. 'The guy's gay. And she's been seeing someone else on and off for weeks, anyway.'

'Has she?' Cat tasted the white wine the waiter had poured for her. She made her voice casual. 'What's he like?'

'Younger than her, of course. Dark, with money. I haven't taken that much notice. Why do you ask?'

She shrugged. 'Just in case he's my next stepfather, of course.' She paused. 'The bouquet at Belinda's wedding. She caught it, remember? And that means she's going to be married.'

He snorted. 'A ridiculous superstition.'

'Maybe,' she said. 'Maybe not.' There was mineral water on the table too, and she drank some because her mouth was so dry. 'I suppose he's good-looking?'

David was looking past her, his eyes narrowed, his mouth a taut line. He said, 'Well, you can judge for yourself, my sweet. He and your mother have just walked in. We can have a nice family party.' He grated out the words.

Cat found herself putting her glass down very carefully. There'd been a queen called Cat once, she thought. One of Henry's wives, back in the sixteenth century—Cat Howard, who'd been executed. And twenty-first-century Cat suddenly knew exactly what it must have been like to put your head on the block and wait for the axe to fall.

'David.' Vanessa appeared beside them, smiling. 'And my

lovely Cathy. What a wonderful surprise.' She turned to the man beside her. 'Darling, you remember my daughter, don't you? And this, of course, is David, who used to be my favourite leading man.' She gave her enchanting gurgle of laughter. 'David—meet Liam Hargrave.'

CHAPTER ELEVEN

CAT was frozen. All her worst fears had been suddenly—terribly—justified, and the ice inside her had reached her throat—her face. She was afraid if she tried to speak—to move her lips—nothing would happen.

She looked up into Liam's cool, expressionless face. No embarrassment, she realised, and no regret. And no desire in his eyes, either, or longing that had to be sated. Just a faint wariness.

He thinks I might scream, she thought, or faint. Make some kind of dreadful scene. Throw wine. Fall on my knife...

He said, 'Good evening, Miss Adamson. We seem to keep meeting in restaurants.'

Three times, she thought dazedly. We've met this way three times before. Third time lucky—isn't that what they say? And now she could have screamed. Could feel it welling up inside her, heartbroken and almost uncontrollable. Almost, but not quite.

She said, 'Don't worry, Mr Hargrave. I can guarantee it won't happen again.' And turned away.

She watched him shake hands with her father, their eyes meeting like duellists before a fight to the death.

Only she was the one who was dying.

I did this, she thought. Because I was scared, and I had to know why. Had to find out. So I tried to use my own father, and I've been punished for it. Dear God, have I been punished.

'Maybe we could all sit together?' Vanessa was looking round. 'Shall we ask them to arrange it?'

Oh, God, no. Please—no.

'We're in the middle of our meal, Van,' David said quietly. 'Another time, perhaps.'

'Well,' she said. 'You're probably right.' She looked up at Liam, sliding her arm through his. 'Darling, we'd better go to our table.'

She didn't watch to see where they went. Everything had to appear normal. She forked up a scallop and ate it, aware that David was watching her, frowning a little.

'You know him, do you—this Liam Hargrave?'

'I've met him,' she said. 'But I don't know him.' *And I never will...*

'Hmm.' His frown deepened. 'This one looks as if he has a brain as well. Perhaps it is serious, for once.'

Cat put down her fork. 'Very likely,' she said, and felt herself begin to weep inside.

It was the most difficult meal she'd ever endured. She made a pretence of eating the guinea fowl that followed, but most of it stayed on her plate, and she swiftly declined all offers of dessert or coffee.

She wanted to be out of there. She wanted to be on her own, so that she could howl her despair at the moon.

Fortunately, her father didn't seem disposed to linger either, and they managed to pick up a passing cab on the corner.

Apart from her asking if she could be dropped off first, they held very little conversation. And as soon as she reached her flat Cat ran to the bathroom and was violently sick. Even when her stomach was empty she carried on retching miserably, head spinning and tears running down her face.

Liam and Vanessa, she thought. Vanessa and Liam.

It couldn't be happening. It was another nightmare, it had to be, and soon she would wake and he would hold her and comfort her.

'I'm here now,' he'd said, and if she'd listened properly she might have heard the implicit warning in his words. Because he'd been telling her he wouldn't be there for ever— or not for her anyway.

And now he'd never be with her again, even though he was the only man she would ever love.

There, she thought, I've admitted it at last, just when all hope is gone.

It wasn't a sudden revelation. If she was honest she'd known from the first that he was different, but she'd fought against that knowledge bitterly—desperately. Telling herself over and over again that it wasn't love but sex that she wanted. The act of love rather than the act of loving.

Two people, she thought, having the faith to make vows and keep them—to build a life together. And she'd deliberately thrown the chance of that away. Destroyed her future happiness with both hands. Because she wouldn't listen to what her heart was telling her.

'I didn't want the truth,' she whispered. 'I wanted the stupid fantasy I'd invented, and now I have nothing.'

She'd even given Liam the licence to choose elsewhere. But she'd never, even in her worst moments, dreamed his choice would be Vanessa. His boyhood goddess, she thought with a faint moan. Still beautiful—still fascinating. Still stealing hearts.

He told me I was beautiful, she thought desolately. And although I knew it wasn't true I loved to hear him say it.

But he never once said he loved me. At least he played fair about that, although it's small consolation now.

And I never said I loved him, either.

So often the words had been there, urging her to speak them. To admit that she wanted all of him—body and soul—the whole package. To be his wife if he asked her. To make the leap of faith gladly with him.

But would it have made any real difference if she'd done so? she asked herself sadly. Or would Vanessa still have taken him, leaving her with the knowledge that she'd simply humbled herself for nothing?

Maybe she'd spared herself an even greater misery than she was experiencing now.

She shed her clothing and crawled into bed, hugging her arms round her shivering body.

In a few hours she would have to get up, dress, and go to work, pretending that her life hadn't ended and not being able to talk about it to anyone. Because the only shoulder it was possible for her to cry on was Liam's. And he no longer wanted her.

I can't go on thinking like this, she told herself, *or I shall go mad.*

She had to start being rational—practical. She needed to dispose of all the things he'd given her, for a start, then she'd remove his number from her mobile phone, after which she'd take back the keys to the flat and leave them there.

She would behave well, she thought, and then he would never know how close she'd come to cracking. She'd be spared that particular humiliation if nothing else.

She must make him believe that she'd meant what she said. That all she'd wanted was a physical relationship without strings, and with no recriminations when it ended.

And that she'd have no great difficulty in finding someone to take his place.

And if she could manage that, then one day, in the distant future, she might even be able to convince herself.

She'd meant to be brave, but she soon discovered that going back to the flat was a really bad idea. Even as she was parking the car her heart was thudding and her hands were damp.

She was tempted just to put the keys through the letterbox, and run, but she needed to go in and take a last look round, in case she'd been careless and left something. She'd done that sometimes over the past couple of months, although she'd been scrupulous at first about taking anything she'd brought away with her when she left.

In fact, she'd missed an earring, after that last visit, just two nights ago. It wasn't particularly valuable—just one of a favourite pair—and the cleaners might have found it and put it where she couldn't miss it again.

It would only take seconds to look, Cat assured herself, and she could be in and out in no time at all.

She unlocked the door and walked along the passage to the empty sitting room. Only it wasn't empty at all. Liam was sitting on one of the sofas, and he rose as she came in and looked at her.

She checked instantly, her heart pounding and her throat tightening in genuine shock. She said, 'I'm sorry—I didn't realise you'd be here. I—I'll go.'

'Why?' His voice was cool and level. 'You must have had good reason to come back.'

'The best,' she said. 'I need to leave these.'

She held out the keys, and then realised he might come and take them from her hand—that his fingers might brush hers—which would be unthinkable. Unbearable. So she walked to the fireplace and put them on the mantelshelf.

She went on in a little rush, 'And I wanted to have a look round—check I hadn't left any personal stuff inadvertently.'

'You haven't,' he said. 'I've already looked, and there's no trace of you.' The smoky eyes were grave. 'Rules obeyed to the letter. Just as you've always wanted.'

'All the same,' she said, 'I'd like to see for myself. If you don't object?'

His mouth twisted. 'Be my guest—one more time.'

There was no earring in the bathroom or the bedroom. She'd probably lost it somewhere completely different. Anyway, it was gone, and she wouldn't think of it again. Part of all the other things she had to banish from her mind somehow.

What she now had to decide was how, possibly, she could deal with the present situation.

I have to play it cool, she told herself. I may be breaking up inside, but I can't let him see that—can't allow one crack in the façade. My God, my parents are both actors, I must have inherited something in the genes. And I can do this—because I have to. There's no choice.

When she returned to the sitting room Liam had moved to the window, and was standing looking down into the communal garden. As she hesitated in the doorway he turned and their eyes met.

'Don't worry,' she said. 'I'm not going to ask what you're thinking, or if there's a problem. Because I don't have to, do I? It's all been made perfectly clear.'

She paused. 'Why didn't you tell me to my face that it was all over the other night?' She slowed her voice to a drawl. 'Or were you planning to have your cake and eat it too?'

Something came and went in his face, but when he spoke his tone matched her own faintly amused indifference. 'An interesting idea,' he acknowledged. 'What a pity it never occurred to me.'

'Are you quite sure about that?' Cat challenged contemptuously. 'Just as a matter of interest, you understand, when did you first start seeing Vanessa?'

'Does it really matter?' He sounded weary. 'And is it any of your concern, anyway?'

'Yes,' she said, managing not to flinch. 'I—really—think it does matter. Vanessa is, after all, my mother.'

He was silent for a moment. 'Very well,' he said. 'We've been meeting since that day at Vanni's. Does that satisfy your curiosity?'

'Meeting here?' There was a sudden hoarseness in her voice, which might have been a betrayal.

'No,' he said. 'No one has been here apart from you.'

'What a terrible waste,' she said. 'When the place is all set up for—whatever.' She paused. 'Clean sheets on the bed, and towels in the bathroom every day. Total anonymity. Not a sign of—me—anywhere.' She couldn't bring herself to say 'us'.

She added, 'Now you can just—continue the tenancy.'

'No,' he said. 'I shan't keep the flat on.'

'Why not?'

His voice was suddenly hard. 'Because it's outlived its usefulness.'

'Rather like the affair itself,' she said lightly.

'And because I want something better for the woman I love,' Liam went on, as if she hadn't spoken. 'I want to make a home with her. This is not a home, and never will be.'

Pain slashed at her as she shrugged. 'But then it wasn't meant to be.'

'No,' he said. 'It wasn't. And it's fulfilled its purpose very well. Although I think we both knew it couldn't last for ever.' He paused. 'I haven't asked, of course, if you want to keep the flat on yourself. Somewhere to pursue your uncommitted existence,' he added, his lip curling slightly.

'God, no.' She even achieved a laugh. 'When it's over, it's over. And it's just a shell, anyway. There's nothing here.'

She was lying, because the flat wasn't empty at all. It was a network of images. Most of them intimate. All of them disturbing.

Their clothing littering the floor, she thought. Liam in bed, drinking wine with her out of the same glass. Liam watching with sensual appreciation as she stripped for him very slowly. Above all, Liam himself, naked. That beloved, precious, exciting body that she would never touch again.

Those pictures would haunt her for ever, she thought, the breath catching in her throat. Together with the tone of his voice, the smooth warmth of his skin, and the integral, unique scent of him.

'No,' he said. 'You're right. There's nothing. Which is precisely why I intend to give it up and find somewhere else. A place where I can make a life of my own, with a woman of my own.'

'How cosy,' Cat said, wanting to hurt him as badly as she was hurting. 'But I hope you're not planning on being a family man. I don't think my mother could quite manage that.'

'On the contrary,' he said coldly. 'She's perfectly able to

have another child if she chooses. Women older than her do it all the time.'

No, she screamed at him silently. You can't say that—you can't even think it. Because I'm the one who should be having your children, and no one else. Any alternative would be obscene. It's got to be me and only me—or else how can I bear it?

'Heavens,' she said, with an exaggerated widening of the eyes. 'You mean this has actually been discussed?'

'We've talked about a lot of things.'

'I can imagine.' She hesitated. 'Does she know about all this?' She gestured around her. 'Have you told her about us—about the deal?'

'Do you want me to?' His gaze met hers, coldly, directly.

'No,' she said. 'I see no necessity for that. We've been discreet and kept it secret, so let it stay that way.' She gave a small, hard smile. 'Can you imagine what the press would do if news of the mother and daughter show ever got out? Not all publicity is good publicity, believe me, not even for my parents.'

'I bow,' Liam said, 'to your superior judgement.' He walked to the mantelpiece and pocketed the keys. 'Is there anything else?' he asked. 'Or do we call it a day?'

'I can't think of a thing.' Cat threw back her head, letting her eyes travel slowly down his body. 'Unless you fancy one last encounter, of course,' she added, keeping her tone jokey. 'The bed's waiting. We could say goodbye in style.'

And if that doesn't convince him that all I cared about was the sex, nothing will.

'Thank you,' he said politely, with no answering amusement in his eyes. 'But, strangely enough, I always promised myself that when I finally met the woman I wanted for my wife I would love her and remain faithful to her for the rest of my life. But I appreciate the kind offer.'

Cat bit her lip hard. 'Then—I hope you'll be—happy.' She kept her voice steady by a superhuman effort, the rusty taste of blood in her mouth. 'Cheers,' she said brightly. 'And—thanks for the memory. All the memories.'

His own voice was very quiet. 'Goodbye—Catherine.'

She made it out of the flat and into the road, her head high. It was only when she was back in her car, a street away, with the doors locked, that she allowed the agony of grief to have its way with her at last. Whispering, 'I've lost him for ever,' over and over again, as the tears poured down her numb face.

Why wasn't amnesia available on the health service? There were specialist clinics for everything, so why couldn't she book in somewhere and say, Please erase the last three months?

She'd always been sparing with cosmetics, but now each morning she painted her face like an artist, trying to recreate a girl called Cat Adamson, who'd thought that she could have a life without love and marriage. Someone who'd insisted on her independence and was now stuck with it.

Someone who laughed and talked and met with clients, as if it actually mattered. And who was managing, somehow, to hide the fact that she was dying inside.

It had occurred to her that she might just possibly be expecting Liam's child, and for a brief time she'd allowed herself the sin of hope. After all, protection sometimes failed. Her own birth had been an accident—a glitch in her mother's career, never to be repeated. At least, not until now, when Liam had come into Vanessa's life, making her reevaluate her priorities.

But the course of nature soon dealt briskly with her futile, guilty yearnings, and she tried hard to be thankful.

Apart from the continuing anguish of losing Liam, Cat found Vanessa's phone calls were the most difficult problem to deal with. They would never have the perfect mother and daughter relationship, but they'd started almost tentatively to become friends. Now Cat had to be on her guard all the time when they spoke, waiting for Liam's name to be mentioned, ready to fence and be evasive. Intent on preventing even a hint of her private agony entering her voice.

Not that he was mentioned that often, and when it happened Vanessa spoke almost casually, as if he was simply an accepted part of her life.

However, she seemed far more concerned with *Playwright in Residence* and the difficulties Sharine was causing as opening night approached, than she seemed to be with her love affair.

'She dried four times in her first scene last night,' Vanessa said irritably during one conversation. 'And she missed an exit cue, of all things. Stood there as if she'd been superglued to the stage. And it's the dress rehearsal tomorrow,' she added with a groan.

'How's my father taking it all?' Cat asked, intrigued in spite of herself.

'With amazing tolerance,' Vanessa said acerbically. 'Either that or he's lost the will to live.' She paused. 'Now, you are coming to the opening night, darling, aren't you? You can watch us being booed off the stage.'

Cat hesitated. 'I'm not sure,' she said evasively. 'I'm having to work late a great deal. Times are really hard just now, and we're tendering for everything these days.'

'Oh, but you must come. We need one friendly face in the audience.' Vanessa paused. 'Besides, there's a party afterwards, so I'll leave your ticket at the box office, shall I? Must dash, sweetie. See you later.'

Cat sighed as she switched off her phone. There was no question of her attending the party, but no matter what excuse she made, and how valid it was, both parents would be hurt if she didn't show up at the theatre for the performance.

I may not have a choice here, she thought ruefully.

But when Thursday evening came she was still at her desk, working on an estimate and completely undecided on how to spend her evening.

'Oh, you're here. Excellent.' Andrew appeared beside her. 'I may have some good news for a change.'

He rubbed his hands almost gleefully. 'We've been approached by the Durant hotel chain. Smallish, classy and exclusive—you know the kind of thing. Lately they've been moving into some of the top resorts in Europe and the Caribbean, but now they're focusing on their British market again, and planning a big refurbishment programme. And they've asked us to put in a bid for the work.' He whistled. 'Tell you what, Cat, if we get it, it'll be a real feather in our collective caps.' He paused. 'Ever stayed in a Durant hotel?'

'Yes, as it happens,' Cat said slowly. 'My cousin had her wedding reception at one of them—a place called Anscote Manor.'

'And?'

Cat shrugged. 'There were a few snags at Reception, but the rest of it seemed lovely. I didn't feel it needed much improvement.' Or nothing that we can arrange anyway, she added silently.

'Well, the Durant board clearly doesn't agree with you,' Andrew said briskly. 'Because Anscote Manor's the first on the list for treatment, and I want you to go down there on a preliminary visit next week.'

Cat listened in dismay. Anscote Manor was number one on her list too, she thought grimly—of places to avoid. She couldn't return there with her memories. She just couldn't...

She hesitated. 'Couldn't someone else do it? I—I do have quite a lot on.'

'You have a reasonable amount,' said Andrew. 'Spread pretty thinly, and you know it. Cat, we need this contract. It could be so big for us. Besides, they asked for you. Said complimentary things about your work on the London Phoenix last year.'

'The London Phoenix had been a hostel and was practically derelict,' Cat pointed out drily. 'Simply dynamiting it would have been an improvement.'

'Then this will be a walk in the park,' said Andrew, in a voice that suggested further argument was futile. He glanced at his watch. 'And shouldn't you be gone by now? I thought you were going to the theatre.'

Cat chewed her lip, her mind still on Anscote Manor and the inevitable memories it brought to mind.

'Yes,' she said reluctantly. 'I suppose I must.'

She hadn't brought a change of clothes, so her working gear—a plain black suit with a knee-length skirt, and a long-sleeved white blouse—would have to do, she thought, as she applied some lipstick in the back of the taxi.

She only just made it. The house lights were already going down as she edged along the row to her stall seat. But it was not too dark to recognise her immediate neighbour and stop dead in her tracks, hardly able to breathe.

'Good evening,' Liam said courteously.

'Is this some sick joke?' Cat asked, recovering the power of speech with an effort.

'Of course not.' There was a touch of impatience in his voice. 'You must have known I'd be here tonight.' He paused. 'Is it a problem for you?'

If she said yes and walked out, then he'd know in an instant how much he mattered to her, and any small advantage she'd gained from their last meeting would be lost.

On the other hand, the prospect of spending the evening within touching distance of him was a major nightmare, and she was shaking already.

'I suggest you sit down,' he went on. 'The curtain's about to go up, and they've announced a change in the programme. Mary Fitton's now being played by someone called Jana Leslie.'

The understudy, Cat thought as she subsided silently into her seat, tucking her elbows in at her sides and keeping her knees primly together to reduce the possibility of contact between them.

Under cover of the applause for the set, she said, 'Was this—neighbourly touch—Vanessa's idea?'

'Well, it certainly wasn't mine,' Liam said crushingly, and joined in the clapping for Vanessa's first entrance. 'Don't forget, she would see no reason not to put us together,' he added drily.

She said almost inaudibly, 'I suppose not.'

As the minutes passed Cat began to relax and start to enjoy the play, almost in spite of herself. She could see exactly why her father and mother had opted to do it, not letting their personal acrimony stand in their way. It was a bold and witty script, and the dialogue fizzed and sparkled. In spite of the emotional turmoil raging inside her, Cat found herself laughing out loud.

Understudy Jana Leslie was a beautiful girl and a natural brunette. If she was nervous at finding herself on stage on opening night she didn't let it show, and she gave an accomplished performance.

'I think a star might be born,' Liam commented as the curtain descended for the interval.

'You could be right.' She kept her voice neutral. 'Did they say why Sharine wasn't appearing?'

'No,' he said. 'I suspect the rest of the cast have murdered her and stuffed the body up that huge chimney on the set.' He paused. 'I've ordered you a white wine in the bar,' he added. 'I hope that's what you want?'

She looked at him incredulously. 'You mean you knew I was coming?'

'I certainly hoped you would,' he said. 'I wouldn't like Vanessa to be disappointed.' He gave Cat a steady look. 'Are you coming for this drink?'

'No,' Cat said. 'Thank you. I prefer to stay here.'

His mouth tightened. 'Just as you wish.' As he departed he brushed against her slightly, and Cat felt herself flinch.

The auditorium seemed to be emptying fast, few people remaining. As Vanessa and David's daughter, she was going to be conspicuous. She sat for a moment, nerving herself, then rose and followed him.

This was a social occasion and she needed to behave socially, whatever the personal cost.

She caught up with him in the bar. 'I'm sorry, that was ungracious.' She mustered a smile. 'I must be tired. It's been a tricky day at work.'

'Well, they happen.' He retrieved their drinks and passed Cat's wine to her.

'The play's terrific, isn't it?' She looked around, nodding. 'And they're enjoying it. My parents always said you could judge by the reaction of the interval crowd, and they're all talking and laughing. It's going to be a big success.' She took a deep breath. 'And Vanessa's brilliant. Will you let her know that I said so, please?'

'Why don't you tell her yourself?'

She was aware of him watching her over the top of his glass, and flushed. 'Because I'm not coming to the party.'

'Ah,' he said. 'Still staying aloof and walking alone. That's what you do best, isn't it, Cat?'

'Even if it were true,' she said, 'it's no longer your concern. Kindly remember that.' She raised her glass. 'Happy days.'

His smile was mocking. 'Not to mention nights,' he said softly, and drank.

She'd used to wonder how it would be to go to the theatre with him—have a drink together in public. Well, now she knew, and it was sheer hell.

She put her glass down carefully on a ledge. 'I don't think I'm thirsty after all,' she said. 'And I might also give act two a miss. I hope you don't mind.'

'You don't want to find out what happens?'

'I know how it ends,' Cat said. 'Unhappily, like so many things in life. I'm good at endings.'

As she turned to walk away he put a hand on her arm, halting her.

'Cat.' His voice had suddenly changed—become strained

and urgent. 'Cat, don't go—not like this. We really need to talk.'

She stepped back, wrenching herself free, disregarding the surprised and inquisitive glances around her.

She said in a low voice which throbbed with anger, 'Don't touch me. Do not dare to touch me. Because I'm off limits to you, now and always, and all the talking's been done.'

She paused, lifting her chin. 'I really hope that things work out between you and my mother. But please note I'm not expecting an invitation to the wedding—and just don't ever ask me to call you Father.'

And she turned and walked away from him, without looking back.

CHAPTER TWELVE

THE reviews for the play that week bordered on rapturous, hailing the revival of the old Carlton/Adamson magic. David and Vanessa had a hit on their hands, and Jana Leslie's career was launched.

Cat had to be pleased for all of them. She was only glad that no one had witnessed the other small drama being played out in the bar during the interval.

And it seemed she was not the only member of the family to have suffered a blow to the heart. Her father, too, was on his own again.

It was ironic, she thought. The play was a tremendous success—a smash hit completely sold out for months. Yet it was a triumph that had cost David his Sharine.

It had been an acute attack of stage fright on her part that had sent Jana Leslie on in her place that first night, and the understudy had played the role ever since, while Sharine made hysterical scenes, brandishing doctors' notes about her emotional state and accusing the entire cast of being against her. And, as Vanessa had tartly commented, if they hadn't been at the start, they certainly were in the end.

The production company had finally offered her one last chance to appear in the Mary Fitton role, and when she'd refused had torn up her contract. In turn, Sharine had flounced back to California, threatening law suits and confidently expecting David to follow.

But he had not pursued her. As in the play, so in real life. The theatre had won in the end. There was no way her father was going to give up a part as good as this, especially when people were talking about awards.

But the Sharine affair had taken its toll on him, she thought.

Since her departure his unhappiness had been palpable, and he spent more and more time in his dressing room alone.

He didn't even want to talk about it, which was uncharacteristic of her father, who liked to wring as much emotion out of his personal dramas as he did from the stage variety.

'I let her go,' he said to Cat over lunch one day, when she'd asked him diffidently how things were going. 'I let her go, and now I've lost her. Every hope I ever had is gone.' For a moment he stared into space, his face harsh. 'How could I have been such a fool?'

'Dad.' She put her hand gently on his, feeling his pain as acutely as she did her own, but he rallied instantly, changing the subject with a kind of dogged determination.

Cat thought privately that David had been lucky to escape, but she couldn't tell him that. It would have been far too cruel. He seemed to have visibly aged, and, whatever her opinion of Sharine, Cat wasn't used to seeing him so despondent. She hated it—although it occurred to her, when she returned to the theatre alone one night, to watch the play in full, that his unhappiness had added a greater depth to his performance.

Vanessa, on the other hand, was as near achieving serenity as Cat had ever seen her. She seemed to be floating on air, while Cat suffered accordingly.

Vanessa had exclaimed reproachfully over her failure to attend the party. 'But I'm going to hold a little private celebration of my own in a week or two,' she confided. 'And you're certainly coming to that. In fact, I won't take no for an answer.'

But she might have to, thought Cat. Especially if the purpose of the occasion was to announce that she and Liam were getting married.

I can't bear it, she told herself, wrapping her arms across her wincing body. I *won't* bear it.

To that end, she'd been making preliminary private enquiries about the prospect of living and working abroad. She didn't want to go, but to stay—to see Liam and Vanessa together and pretend indifference—would be impossible for her. An unendurable thorn in her shrinking flesh.

So Anscote Manor might well be her last project for her present company, and an unwelcome one at that. And she couldn't even sweeten the pill by paying Aunt Susan a visit, because the house was now on the market and she was staying in a villa in Tuscany, with a group of other single women, apparently having a whale of a time.

Building a new life, Cat thought forlornly, from the ashes of her old one. And maybe, one day, I shall have to ask her how it's done.

It was a grey day with rain in the air when Cat eventually drove down to Anscote Manor for the second time. In a way, she was glad of the chill, damp weather. If the sun had been shining it would have been yet another unhappy reminder of times past.

She'd been told to report to a Miss Trevor, who was some kind of executive manager in the Durant hierarchy, and had travelled down specially to discuss the possible changes Cat might propose.

Perhaps it will be good for me psychologically, she thought as she parked her car. If I alter the place enough it won't be part of this dangerous romantic dream of mine any longer. A first step, maybe, in my emotional rehabilitation. And long overdue.

She knew that she had to forget Liam. That she must put him out of her mind entirely. And she wanted to do this. She longed to be able to do it, because she didn't need the searing wretchedness she woke to each morning or the lonely expanse of emptiness in her bed at night.

But everything seemed to conspire against her.

His relationship with her mother put him inevitably at the forefront of her consciousness, and there was no escape from that because Vanessa mentioned him constantly.

It was only a matter of time, surely, before the press got

on to this intriguing new affair for Vanessa Carlton, leading to daily bulletins on its progress, complete with photographs. And leading eventually, she assumed, to the announcement of their engagement.

A bitter pill for her father to swallow too, under the circumstances, she thought wryly. He'd always seemed the more resilient of the two, but there was no sign of his taking an interest in another lady since Sharine's departure.

After every performance he went straight home.

And his only real social life is having lunch with me, Cat thought wryly. How are the mighty fallen.

And, in the meantime, she had plenty of troubles of her own...

She squared her shoulders, took a deep, painful breath, then marched resolutely into the hotel. There was a new receptionist behind the desk, an older woman she hadn't seen before. She was welcoming and pleasant, but almost certainly a much tougher proposition than the other girls, and therefore not easily susceptible to the blandishments of male guests, however attractive.

A change for the better already, Cat thought drily as she made her way, as directed, to the Conference Suite. The double doors were open, and a woman was standing there, tall, slim and young, and tapping her foot impatiently, as if Cat was late, which she wasn't.

She switched on her professional smile. 'Miss Trevor—I'm Catherine Adamson.' And faltered into silence as she realised that she'd seen the foot-tapper before somewhere.

My God, she thought. It's the brunette with the legs. The one who was dining with Liam at Mignonette when I was there with poor Tony. I'd know her anywhere.

And the room felt suddenly colder.

But if Miss Trevor recognised Cat in turn, she wasn't letting on. She merely shook hands in a perfunctory way, gave Cat's workaday pinstripe suit a disdainful look, and twitched the lapel of her own designer jacket.

'I'm doing the initial briefing,' she announced. 'But you'll actually be dealing directly with our chairman. He's very interested in this particular project, and he will naturally make any final decision about the awarding of contracts.'

Cat murmured something and seated herself in the chair indicated, opening her briefcase with a growing sense of foreboding. She ought to respond with some polite and positive remark, and she knew it, but her brain seemed to have stopped working. Because, unless she'd descended into total paranoia, she knew exactly who would be walking into the conference room next. And suddenly her hands were clammy, her entire senses vibrating nervously.

'Apparently your firm comes highly recommended.' Miss Trevor sounded dubious. 'But the Durant chain has very exacting standards.'

'I know that,' Cat said, hanging on to her professional calm by a thread. 'I spent the night here once.' She paused. 'On the whole, my impressions were good.'

From behind her, Liam said, 'Only on the whole? In what respect did you feel we let you down, Miss Adamson?'

She did not look round. Every vertebra in her spine seemed locked in sudden tension as her worst fear was confirmed.

'It was human error,' she returned. 'Rather than the ambience of the hotel itself. Computer systems crashing with a resulting breakdown in data security—that kind of thing.'

'The computer system has been changed,' he said softly. 'I hope you find that reassuring.'

'I'm here as a design consultant,' she said. 'Not a guest. And my remit does not include your software.'

Miss Trevor gave a slight indrawn breath. She clearly thought this an inappropriate exchange. 'Shall I take Miss Adamson on a tour of the principal rooms?' she suggested. 'Explain the board's vision to her?'

'I think Miss Adamson already knows what's involved,' Liam drawled. 'And as I'm here, Sandra, I may as well take over. Perhaps you could arrange some coffee for us?'

'Nothing for me, thanks,' Cat denied curtly. She got up slowly and faced Liam, her body taut in challenge. 'Are you quite sure about the need for this refurbishment programme, Mr Hargrave? I had the idea the hotel had been redecorated quite recently anyway.'

'The name is Durant,' Liam said softly. 'Hargrave is my middle name.'

'I'm sorry,' she said huskily. 'Clearly I've been—misinformed.'

'Don't worry about it,' he said. 'These mistakes happen.' He paused. 'As to the décor, in spite of what may have been done, I feel there are a number of rooms in the hotel that are not quite up to standard. Shall we go and take a look?'

He turned to Miss Trevor. 'Sandra, maybe you should come with us and make notes so there are no further misapprehensions,' he suggested gently. 'I thought we'd start with the restaurant, and then move on to a typical bedroom.' He paused. 'Room Ten, perhaps.'

Cat reached numbly for her briefcase, realising too late it was open and watching the papers inside cascade over the floor. But at least the effort of bending to retrieve them explained the heated flush in her face. Or she hoped it might.

Somehow she had to regain some ground, although any possibility of obtaining the Durant contract was history and she knew it. But what could have prompted him to set up this farcical situation in the first place? She ached inside from the cruelty of it.

'You have a reason for choosing that particular room?' she asked, with a coolness she was far from feeling, as they ascended the stairs and walked along the corridor.

'I want to ensure that all our guests leave here with wonderful memories.' His brief smile did not reach his eyes. 'I'm not certain that Room Ten fulfils that for everyone.'

'But probably the average guest isn't quite as exacting as you.'

Liam shook his head. 'The kind of guest I'm thinking of isn't average at all. I'd describe them as highly demanding.'

'And I'm sure the Durant chain is well able to cope,' she said icily, trying to hang on to her temper and control the hurt at the same time. 'At least in the short term.' She came to a halt. 'Would you like me to be honest, Mr Durant?'

'I'd be delighted,' he said. 'I find it a rare quality these days.'

'Then try this for size.' She ignored Sandra Trevor, standing with her mouth open. Faced Liam, her chin raised. 'I think Anscote Manor is fine just as it is. I don't believe it needs any refurbishment, and nor do you. And, as I'm really not interested in playing games, I plan to return to London right now. But don't worry. I won't bill you for my wasted time.'

'On the contrary, I'm perfectly serious, but I can't have made my wishes clear.' He turned to the other girl. 'Would you leave us alone please, Sandra, for a few minutes, while I try and talk Miss Adamson round?'

'There's no need for that,' Cat snapped. 'This isn't the kind of project that would interest my firm, anyway, so there's really no more to be said.' She drew a breath. 'As for Room Ten, I suggest a minimalist look. Everything painted white— bland and instantly forgettable. Now, excuse me, please.' And she wheeled round, her head high, and walked back to the stairs.

When she reached her car she was shaking like a leaf caught in a storm. But he hadn't followed her, she thought as she fumbled the key into the ignition. At least she'd been spared that, if nothing else.

She punched the steering wheel with a clenched fist. What he'd done was unforgivable. He'd been deliberately goading her, forcing her to revisit territory that should have been forbidden for any number of reasons. And only the presence of the po-faced Sandra had prevented her from telling him so, and calling him a bastard.

What the hell was he playing at—getting her down here—

deliberately reminding her of what it had once been like between them? she wondered raggedly. Did he really think she could forget so soon? Did he not know how this would make her feel, or did he not care?

Oh, God, how could he do this? she asked herself, fighting back the incipient tears that threatened her.

Because it wasn't only her emotions that were involved here. Andrew had been excited—keyed up by the approach from Durant—and the firm badly needed the work. There'd been a lot riding on this visit, and she'd blown it away.

And, with equal importance, where was Vanessa in all this? she wondered, staring sightlessly through the windscreen. Presumably she trusted Liam—believed in his commitment to her. But how serious was he? Had he even told her his real identity, or did she still think he was Liam Hargrave?

If she does, should I tell her that she's being deceived, or should I stay out of it, she asked herself. Because there's more than just surnames involved here.

Her mother clearly believed she had found lasting love. So how would she feel about her lover inventing a pretext to meet with his former mistress, and indulging himself with that kind of blatant sexual teasing?

He told me he intended to be faithful to the woman he loved, she thought bitterly. But today's performance hardly bodes well for the future.

And if she'd gone with him to Room Ten would he have stopped at mere words? And how would she have reacted if he had sent Sandra Trevor away and started to make love to her in earnest?

Her whole body quivered at the thought of his mouth on hers, his hands touching her starved flesh—rousing her. And she despised herself for it. Because he was no longer hers to desire. He had turned away from her to Vanessa, and she would not allow her mother to be hurt just because he fancied a little cynical dalliance with an old flame.

I hate him, she thought, swallowing back her tears. But at

the same time I can't stop loving him—and I know I never will. He has me, body, heart and soul. And how sad and crazy is that?

And now I have to drive back to London and tell Andrew the bad news.

She sighed as she started the car, because she knew that in spite of everything she would not say a word to Vanessa.

Instead she would take steps to distance herself from Liam Hargrave Durant.

As far as possible, she thought. And for as long as it takes.

As the seat-belt light came on Cat slipped her paperback into her bag and leaned back with a little sigh. The captain had said it was a perfect autumn day in London, which meant it would probably feel cold after three weeks in St Lucia.

But, all the same, she was glad to be back. She'd had a wonderfully relaxed time, swimming and snorkelling in the perfect sea. She'd spent several astonishing days sightseeing, too. And, even though she'd carefully monitored her sunbathing, she'd managed to acquire a light honey tan.

She looked good, and she felt good too. And, best of all, she was ready to take control of her life again.

Not that she was cured of Liam by any means, she admitted unwillingly. She knew now that it was never going to be that easy. He still occupied her waking thoughts and sleeping dreams at a dangerous level. But each time he came into her mind now she tried to block him—to focus with single-minded determination on something else. Only time would tell if this would have any permanent effect, but she could always hope. Couldn't she?

And, of course, if Liam's affair with Vanessa had somehow run aground during her absence he might be out of her life altogether.

And that would make the perfect end to a perfect holiday, she told herself firmly, ignoring the fist clenching in her stomach.

She hadn't intended to have a break at all, of course.

After her abortive trip to Anscote Manor she'd worried all the way back to London over how to tell Andrew she'd failed even to acquire the right to bid for the Durant contract. And what excuse could she give for her unprofessional behaviour in walking out on a potential client? Somehow she hadn't thought a plea of extreme provocation would get her off the hook. Not without tortuous and potentially embarrassing explanations.

But to her amazement he'd reacted philosophically, and refused point-blank to accept her offer to resign.

'Things are going to get better,' he told her. 'I trust my instincts. And I was wrong to dump the Durant thing on you, when I could see you were already working flat out.' He gave her a searching look. 'You've been looking really tired lately, honey, and I should have done something about it. You've got holiday piling up, so why don't you find an island somewhere and grab some late sun?'

'Yes,' she said slowly. 'It would be good to get right away for a while. It might clear my head—give me a new perspective on things.'

'Sally and I went to St Lucia a couple of years ago and we loved it,' Andrew said.

'Then I'll try there first,' she said. 'But anywhere will do.' *As long as it doesn't have a Durant hotel,* she added silently.

And, as there wasn't a sign of one on St Lucia, that was where she'd gone.

And she would say to everyone who asked, I had a great time, and pretend that it didn't matter that she'd found herself alone and lonely in a world of couples. And tell herself that the words 'might have been' had never occurred to her.

Her answering machine was winking furiously when she let herself into her flat. She dropped her luggage in the sitting room and listened to her messages. There was only one demanding urgent attention, and that was from her mother.

So that had to be her priority, she thought with a faint sigh as she dialled the number.

Vanessa answered at once, as if she'd been sitting by the phone. 'Darling,' she said. 'You're back at last. How marvellous. Did you have a wonderful time?'

'Yes,' Cat acknowledged. 'It's a fantastic place, and the weather was glorious.' She paused, aware that there was a note of suppressed excitement in her mother's voice which had nothing to do with her return. 'How are things with you?' she went on, more slowly.

Vanessa sighed, almost rapturously. 'Absolutely wonderful. I don't think I've ever been as happy in my life.' She lowered her voice mysteriously. 'What are you doing at ten a.m. the day after tomorrow?'

Cat looked ruefully about her. 'Laundry, I suspect. Also vacuuming. Why?'

'Because I'd like you to be my bridesmaid.'

There was a sudden roaring in Cat's ears. She found herself on her knees, with the receiver clutched so tightly in her hand that the knuckles had turned white.

She said, 'Did you say—bridesmaid?'

Vanessa laughed. 'Yes, my sweet. I'm getting married very quietly at our local registry office and naturally I want you to be there for me, as one of the witnesses. So will you?'

'Married?' Cat repeated almost helplessly. 'When did you decide this?'

'About two weeks ago. Oh, darling, it's all incredible. I never dreamed I could be so happy—not after all this time.'

The pain inside her was taking Cat's breath—her ability to speak. She'd known this was a possibility—of course she had—but now it was a cruel and bitter reality.

She was afraid to make a sound in case she began moaning Liam's name.

'Catherine?' Vanessa said more sharply. 'Cathy, are you there?'

'Yes.' Her voice cracked. 'I'm happy for you, Mother, but don't you think you might be—rushing this a little?'

'Rushing it?' Vanessa echoed. 'On the contrary, I was desperately afraid that I'd blown it. Left it far too late.' She paused. 'I know it must be rather a shock for you, darling, but promise me that you'll come.'

The palm of Cat's free hand was hurting. She unclenched it and saw a small row of red crescents where her nails had savaged her flesh.

Her voice sounded unnaturally calm. 'I don't really know what to say. After all, the bridegroom might not be too happy to have your grown-up daughter there in attendance.'

'But what nonsense. Of course we both want you,' Vanessa declared. 'You of all people.' She sighed. 'Although Liam did say you probably wouldn't come.'

Cat stiffened. He was daring her, she thought. Challenging her to watch him marry her mother. In fact, he was telling her obliquely that he didn't think she had the guts to face such a thing.

And he was right. She would rather run away screaming than be a witness at his wedding, but for her own self-respect she had to prove him wrong. Or she would never be able to face him again under any circumstances.

She said crisply, 'Then he's wrong. I'd be honoured to be your bridesmaid. What do you want me to wear?'

'Well, I'll be in a cream suit. It's not new, because I haven't had time to look, but I've always loved it, and it's been lucky for me in the past.' Vanessa paused. 'What about that pretty turquoise and ivory dress you wore at Belinda's wedding? Then you can be my "something blue",' she added, inspired.

'Very well,' Cat said slowly, pain wrenching at her as she realised she was to be spared nothing. 'If that's what you'd like.'

'And no wedding presents,' Vanessa decreed. 'That would be silly. It's just going to be a simple ceremony where we declare our love for each other.' She giggled breathlessly. 'I know it's ridiculous, but I'm as nervous as a kitten already. I'll call you tomorrow, darling, to fix the final details.' And she was gone.

Cat put down the phone and tried to get to her feet, but her legs would not support her so she remained where she was. Her skin felt stone-cold, and nausea churned in her stomach.

She'd been so proud of herself as she flew into Heathrow, she thought with dazed bitterness. She'd actually believed that she might be starting to rebuild her life. Taking the first steps to conquer her feelings for Liam.

Well, she knew better now. Every glimpse of him, every mention of his name, was going to be torture for her.

She loved him more than her own life, and she could not have him because, in her blind stupidity and pride, she had never let him see how she felt about him. And now it was too late.

Because in two days' time she would have to stand behind her own mother and smile, and pretend she was not dying inside. And it would have to be the greatest acting performance of all time if she was to get away with it.

'How do I look?' Vanessa demanded for the umpteenth time. She produced a mirror from her bag and scrutinised her flawless complexion.

'You look wonderful,' Cat, seated beside her in the taxi, reassured her quietly. 'And amazingly beautiful. Your—your husband's going to be so proud,' she added huskily.

There were sudden tears in Vanessa's eyes, and she took Cat's hand and squeezed it convulsively.

'Thank you for this, darling,' she whispered. 'I know I don't deserve it, because I've been a hellish mother. I've made so many mistakes, and now it seems as if I'm being forgiven for them all. Given a whole new chance at life. Real life.'

Cat put a gentle arm round her shoulders and hugged her carefully, so as not to crush the cream suit.

And I've made one mistake, she thought unhappily. And

I'm going to be punished for it for the rest of my days. Starting off with this dress that I've been made to wear. I should have said that I'd thrown it away, or that the cleaners ruined it. Something—anything—rather than have to wear it again—this bitter reminder of the day I first met Liam.

She stared down at the posy of cream roses she was to carry for the ceremony, her eyes blurring. She'd done her best with concealer, blusher, and even eyedrops, but she still looked pale and hollow-eyed through lack of sleep and sheer misery.

Hopefully, she thought, she might be able to hide behind Vanessa's radiance.

Liam was the first person she saw as she walked behind her mother into the foyer of the registry office, and her heart seemed to stop.

He was wearing a dark grey suit with a blue silk tie, and a single rosebud in his buttonhole, and she stood, helpless and wretched, as Vanessa walked towards him, smiling, her hands outstretched.

He was going to take her hands and draw her close and kiss her. Cat knew it. Knew too that any attempt to camouflage her longing and devastation would be all in vain. That anyone could read how she felt for him in her white anguished face.

That here, finally, there was nowhere for her to hide.

She turned and headed blindly for the nearest door. It had to be the waiting room, because there were chairs round the walls and magazines on a central table. And as she closed the door behind her and leaned against it she realised that the room was already occupied. That her father was rising from one of the hard-looking chairs and coming to meet her.

'Darling, what are you doing in here?'

She drew a sharp breath, staring at him in disbelief. 'Shouldn't that be my question?'

He gave her a rueful grin. 'Naturally, I'm keeping a low

profile.' He paused. 'But surely your place is with your mother?'

Cat said in a low voice, 'Yes, I suppose it is. But—unlike you, apparently—I've realised I can't go through with it. That I can't stand there and witness this marriage when it's breaking my heart.' She choked out the words.

David stopped and looked at her, his smile fading into anxiety. He said, 'I hoped you'd be pleased. That you'd see it was right—and even wonderful.' He hesitated, his hands moving in the first awkward gesture of his career. 'That although you might find it a shock you'd still give it your blessing.'

'No,' she said. 'That's just not possible.' She shook her head. 'You'll have to make some excuse for me, Daddy. Pretend I'm ill and have had to leave. Because I don't want to hurt Mummy and spoil her special day.'

'And what about my feelings?' David Adamson said sharply. 'Or don't they count?'

'Of course they do. How can you ask?' Cat could taste the acid of tears in her throat. 'That's why I find it so hard to understand why you're here. How you can bear it.'

'Well,' her father said, with a wry twist of the lips, 'it wouldn't be much of a marriage without the groom.' He paused. 'And I won't pretend I'm not disappointed, Cathy,' he added with a touch of heaviness. 'But if you really find the whole idea so unacceptable, then I'll make up some story to pacify your mother.' He sighed. 'Liam, of course, will be a different problem. He has a lot riding on this wedding. I don't know how he's going to take your walking out on him.'

There was a strange buzzing in Cat's ears. Her lips moved, but no sound emerged.

David looked at her with real concern. 'My dear child, are you all right?'

A voice she did not recognise as hers said in a husky whisper, 'I don't understand what you're saying—what's happening here...'

'Your mother and I are getting married again.' He took both her hands in his. 'Please try to be happy for us.'

'But it can't be true,' Cat said hoarsely. 'You love Sharine—you can't bear life without her. You told me so…'

'I told you?' David shook his head in disbelief. 'Darling, I wasn't talking about Sharine. She was window-dressing, like all the others. Someone to bolster my ego. You see, I've known for a long time that my divorce from your mother was the biggest mistake I'd ever made. I've been through hell, thinking that some other man might make her happier than I had, but I was too proud to let her see it in case she didn't feel the same.'

'But she was seeing Liam,' Cat said numbly. 'She has been for weeks. You must know that.'

'I knew it, all right,' her father said with a touch of grimness. 'I watched them together and felt sick. Once again she seemed to have turned away from me to a younger man. And then a few weeks ago I walked into her dressing room and found them together. He had his arm round her, and she was crying on his shoulder.'

He grimaced. 'I assumed he'd done something to hurt her, and lost it completely. Threatened to punch his lights out— the whole bit. He stayed totally calm, totally in control, and told me it was time that Vanessa and I started talking—being honest with each other. That we'd done enough damage already—especially to you. That because of us you'd developed a phobia about marriage and commitment. That emotionally you wouldn't let him near you, even though you were the only wife in the world that he'd ever want.'

He paused. 'Darling, is that true? Was it our fault?'

Her throat tightened convulsively. 'I think it began there— but there were other factors.' She stopped, looking down blindly at their clasped hands. 'Liam didn't ask me to marry him, Dad. Not ever. He just—walked away.'

'He hoped you'd care enough to follow,' David said gently. 'To give him some sign that you wanted him to stay. Your

mother was the only one who gave him hope. She was convinced that you loved him, but were fighting your true feelings, and that all you needed was time. And, in turn, he reassured her that I wasn't interested in Sharine or anyone else.
But I didn't seem to be interested in her either, and that's why
she was crying when I walked in.'

'So—what happened?'

'He left—and we talked—well, at first anyway.' For a moment her sophisticated father looked almost shy. 'And now
here we are.'

As if on cue there was a tap on the door, and a middle-
aged woman peered in at them. 'The registrar is ready for
you, Mr Adamson,' she said, with a touch of reproof.

'We're coming.' David took a handkerchief from his pocket
and dabbed at Cat's white face. He gave her a grave look.
'Aren't we?'

She hung back. 'I—I—don't know...'

'Do you love him?' David asked sternly.

She looked at him, her lips trembling into a smile. 'Yes.
Oh, yes I do. I—I've been so miserable.'

He kissed her on the forehead. 'Then come and be happy
instead,' he said, and led her out of the room.

She stood rigidly beside Liam, not daring to look at him,
listening almost without hearing as her parents remade their
vows to each other, aware only of him. Of his nearness, and
the abyss that still separated them.

Oh, God, she thought. I love him so desperately, but what
can I say to him? How can we ever put things right between
us?

Then, at the moment when David placed the ring on his
wife's finger, she felt Liam's hand brush hers, and suddenly
her shaking fingers were entwined with his, so warmly, so
tightly, and with such strength that she knew that no words
were needed—no explanations and no excuses—because this
was how they would spend the rest of their lives.

And that her days of walking alone were over for ever.

She looked up at him, her eyes misted, and saw that, although he was smiling, there was a tear on his face too.

'You may kiss the bride,' said the registrar.

Liam turned to her. 'May I?' he whispered, his eyes loving her, longing for her.

'Yes,' said Cat, and went into his arms, lifting her mouth to his.

EPILOGUE

The following September

THE bathroom was lit by candles, their flames burning steadily in the warm, still air.

Cathy tilted the flask of fragrant oil and poured a few drops into the palm of her hand. She began slowly to massage it into her skin, paying particular attention to her breasts and the curve of her stomach.

Music floated in from the bedroom next door, and she leaned back, sighing, letting the warm water caress her, sipping iced mineral water from the carafe on the table beside the bath. Waiting for her mobile phone to ring.

When eventually it did, she picked it up, smiling. 'Darling, at last. You seem to have been gone for ever.'

Her smile widened as she listened. 'You'll be here in twenty minutes? Oh, that's wonderful.' She paused, laying a caressing hand on the gently swelling mound that sheltered his child. 'We'll be waiting for you, my love. Both of us. So hurry—please.'

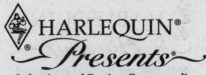